MISTAKEN HERO

RETRIBUTION GAMES BOOK 1

ELLA MILES

RETRIBUTION GAMES SERIES

Mistaken Hero
Forbidden Princess
Tempted Hero
Fatal Princess
Tortured Hero
Dangerous Princess

PROLOGUE
BECKETT

I DID SOMETHING TERRIBLE, the worst. I can't say it, can't even think it. But it's there in my soul and I'll carry it with me forever.

I stare at the dot on my phone's map as I contemplate my next move. I've been watching her location, thinking of all the twisted, fucked up things I want to do to her. I want to murder her, but I also want to fu—*no, I won't even think that.*

The dot starts moving on my phone. At first, I think she's just moving around at the cabin, but then it starts moving faster and quickly ventures beyond the property.

She's running.

No, she wouldn't run. She cares too much.

That only leaves one possibility—she's been kidnapped.

I run to my car with my phone in hand as my anxiety racks through me. There's more at stake than just her, but for a second, all I think of is her safety. My pulse flies thinking about her getting hurt.

I step on the gas as I chase her, but I'm a good hour behind. I call Caius. He answers on the second ring.

"Someone took Ri!" I yell into the phone.

"What? She's—fuck! We're on it."

I hang up the phone, knowing they can track her as well. They are closer, but as I'm already in my car and Caius has to wake the rest of the guys, I'm not sure who will get to her first.

I watch the dot speed toward the city, and I follow, driving like a fucking maniac. I'm sweating, my hand trembling at the wheel. I can't even play music I'm so focused on getting to her.

"I'm going to make it. I'm going to make it. I'm going to make it," I repeat over and over.

When that doesn't work, I repeat, "She's strong. She's strong. She's strong."

The dot suddenly stops.

I look up the address while I speed down the interstate. They took her to a club. And not just any club—the Phantom Brotherhood's club.

They took her.

They rescinded our deal—*those fuckers.*

I step harder on the gas, going as fast as my car will take me. My mind is racing too, and I end up having to take large gulps of air every few seconds because I forget to breathe.

What seems like hours but is actually only a few minutes later, I make it to the club. I don't know what I'm about to walk into, but I'll do whatever it takes to get her back.

I walk through the club as stealthily as possible, so I can scope the place first before drawing attention.

Although that isn't easy to do when you only have one arm, people tend to stare.

I should call the crew and see if they've made it, but when I pull my phone out, I have no reception. I'm not going to waste time going outside to call them, and I'm riled up enough to take down anyone by myself.

I make my way through the main areas and don't find her or any of the Phantom Brotherhood. They must be in a back room.

I head down the hallway when I hear a scream.

It's her.

I can hear it over the booming music—her howl pierces my heart, deflating it like a balloon.

I'm too late. She's been hurt.

I run toward her voice and am led to a locked door. I kick the door down, too impatient to pick the lock. *Their security is shit.*

The sight in front of me rips my heart from my chest.

She's on a pool table naked with four men surrounding her. They are all shirtless, wearing horned masks that make them look like devils or monsters. Most have their dicks out; some have their dicks inside her. *Inside what's mine.*

Except she's not mine. She never will be.

But she's mine to protect.

I see red.

A switch flicks in my brain. I don't think; I just move automatically. The guy that's between her legs—I throw him by the neck and punch him hard in the jaw repeatedly until he's rolling on the floor.

I grab the next one and kick him in the balls. Then a swift kick to the head drops him to his knees.

The third puts up more of a fight, having seen what

I've done to his buddies. He gets a punch into my gut, but it barely slows me down before I knock him out.

And then there's just one. He gets all my remaining rage in the form of punches and kicks. If my outrage was patient, I'd pull a gun out, but luckily for him, I'd rather murder him with my fists.

He doubles over, and her screams are the only thing that keeps me from actually killing him.

She's scared to death, lying naked on the table with a blindfold over her eyes. I can't imagine what is going through her head. The monsters didn't even let her see. They took full advantage of her.

As much as I want to stay around and murder these fuckers, I need to get her out of here.

She removes the mask, and we come face to face. I'm still pissed at her. And it's clear from the way her eyes dilate at my sight that she's pissed at me. But we can be pissed later. I need to get her out of here.

I scoop her up in my arm—not an easy task, but I make it work. I'm not going to throw her over my shoulder when she's in this state. I wish I could cover her better as I head out into the hall, but I'm more worried about those rapists waking up and trying to take her.

Unexpectedly she starts fighting me, beating against my chest and flailing around trying to get out of my arm. I don't know if she thinks I was one of the guys hurting her or if she's mentally still back in that room fighting them off.

I duck into the closest room that will provide some safety until she calms down. I run into a private bathroom, kick the door shut, and turn the lock—only then can I breathe a bit.

"It's okay, Princess. You're safe. I've got you. I won't let them hurt you. You're just in shock." I grip her tighter, but she pushes free.

"What are you doing?"

"Saving you," I say.

"Of course you are, Hero. Of course you are." She runs her hands through her hair with a frustrated grin. "I don't know why you decided to save me this time, but you got one little thing wrong."

I frown, my brows pinching together. "What's that?"

"For once, I didn't need a hero."

"What did you need?"

"I needed you to let me save my damn self."

I cock my head in complete confusion. Somehow I fucked everything up again, but I don't regret it. From where I was standing, she needed a damn hero. I may hate the nickname she gave me as much as she hates me calling her Princess, but I'm not about to stop saving her now, even if it is a mistake.

1

BECKETT

"I DO," Odette says, brightly smiling at me with tears in her eyes.

Those two words take my breath away and have me on the verge of tears. I already succumbed to tears earlier when I watched her walk down the aisle toward me in her sheath white lace dress on her father's arm. I'm the luckiest man in the universe—marrying the woman of my dreams on this perfect spring day in this outdoor Eden.

I've been waiting for this day for the last three months, ever since Odette said yes when I proposed on the rooftop of our favorite building looking out over the Chicago skyline. Three months was as long as I was willing to wait when I've been waiting my entire life for this moment.

I've watched everyone I love get married and have kids. It's finally my turn.

Now there is nothing left standing between us and our happily ever after except the officiant declaring us husband and wife.

I grip Odette's hand tighter like if I loosen my grip, she'll realize her mistake and not marry me after all. Or my real fear—someone will take her from me. A monster will kidnap her, torture her, kill her. When you grew up as I did, it's a very real fear.

She shakes her head knowingly, thinking I'm ridiculous for ever thinking she doesn't want to marry me. I don't know how she could love me—she's an angel and I'm a sinner. She's pure and I'm pure darkness. But somehow, she found a way to love me despite my faults.

"I now declare—" the officiant starts to speak, but suddenly a woman shoulders past him and smacks right into our linked hands, pushing us apart.

"What the hell?" I say, furious at the intruder. We were assured by our wedding planner that the courtyard would be private and secure during the ceremony.

The woman doesn't apologize as she bursts down the aisle, knocking one of the bouquets off the end of a chair. She keeps running frantically as if she's being chased by a dangerous animal, and if she stops for even a second, the animal will catch her and devour her.

I look behind the officiant trying to figure out where she came from and if we can expect more trespassers. But all the doors to the building are closed. Despite how the woman is acting, no one is chasing after her.

I drag my eyes back to the aisle the woman is continuing down. Her raven-colored hair encompasses most of her petite body, but it doesn't hide the small tear on the back of her white buttoned-down blouse, nor the one on the side of her black leggings.

Something happened to her, something cruel. I thought I had left my past behind me. I thought I was free, but it can't be a coincidence that this woman crashed my wedding, *can it?* Not with my history.

It doesn't take a detective to see this woman must work

as a waitress. It explains the outfit and the apron tied around her waist, but not why she's running.

At the last second, she turns around. Her eyes meet mine instantly, ignoring the other hundred people gathered in the courtyard for my wedding.

I expect to see extreme fear in her eyes—terror, maybe. Or at least some anger or rage at what happened to her.

Instead, I see a determination in her large, cat-like eyes that seem to glow with a fierceness I've never seen. She's young, maybe early twenties, but she doesn't carry her youth in her eyes. For a split second, she lets me through her eyes to glimpse what lies beneath—she's an old soul. A tortured one. A dangerous one.

A second later, she turns the corner around the side of the event center and disappears.

I blink rapidly, trying to figure out if I just imagined the interruption entirely when the murmurs of our guests die down almost immediately. Odette once again takes my hand, gripping it with both of hers.

"Well, that will make for a fun memory to tell the kids someday," she jokes.

My eyes race over hers, looking for any sign of distress or annoyance at what just happened, but I find none. Just one of the many reasons why I love her. She doesn't take life too seriously. She's kind and warm and innocent. When she looked at the intruder, she just saw a girl who was a little rude, so she resisted turning into a bridezilla. When I saw the girl, I saw pain, evil, and danger.

I wanted today to be perfect for Odette. She deserves the very best—the wedding day of her dreams.

She notices my concern and strokes my cheek. "Something always goes wrong at weddings. I couldn't have asked for a more perfect day, even with the small interruption. I love you. All I want is to be married to you."

"Shall I continue?" the officiant asks, clearly baffled.

I nod, forcing a smile on my face. There was something odd about that girl, something I'm going to have to explore later, but not now. Now, I need to focus on my wife, on our future. Tomorrow I'll worry about that girl's identity.

"Um...where was I?" the officiant fumbles his note cards.

Odette looks at me with such love in her eyes that it forces me to forget all about the interruption. "You were at the best part, declaring us husband and wife," she says.

I don't wait for him to say it. I dip Odette in my arm and kiss her.

I hear the officiant mumble something about us being husband and wife and kissing the bride, but I don't really hear it. All I hear, feel, and see is her—my wife.

My wife.

My wife.

The kiss warms my entire body, and my mind immediately fills with dirty thoughts of how I'm going to fuck my wife tonight. Odette's face flushes when I break the kiss off, but only after exploring every inch of her mouth with my tongue and making her moan twice.

Our friends and family are hooping and hollering, and I know I let the kiss go on far too long for what's appropriate based on Odette's deep blush. Or maybe she's blushing because she knows what I have planned for her tonight once we get to the penthouse suite I booked.

"No," Odette says as I link our fingers and we start walking down the aisle.

"No, what?" I feign ignorance.

"No, we aren't ditching our wedding reception to go straight to the hotel. My father spent too much money on our wedding to do that."

"I'll write him a check," I wiggle my eyebrows which I know will make her laugh.

She chuckles. "No."

I lean in and kiss her again. I would never deny her the opportunity to celebrate our union with our friends and family, no matter how badly I need her now. My cock is going to be aching all fucking night.

She grabs my tie and yanks my ear to her lips. "But I might be able to be persuaded to a quickie in the bathroom."

I groan and bite the back of my knuckles. "You're trying to kill me."

She knows I won't let our first time as husband and wife be in a dirty bathroom. I want to give her the best of everything, including a magical wedding night with flowers, chocolate-covered strawberries, champagne, the works. A night where I declare my love to her over and over again while I whisper poetic words in her ear. A filthy bathroom won't do.

She knows it, and yet she says it to torture me as if I wouldn't already be thinking about it all night. How could I not when she wears a dress that exposes her entire back and hugs her ass like a vice grip.

A few minutes later, we walk into the ballroom reception. I admit I didn't participate in much of the planning. I don't know what the flowers are called other than 'white.' I don't know about the centerpieces other than they have pops of gold. I don't know about the food, the cake, any of it other than I offered to help pay and plan, but neither she nor her father would hear any of that.

"Ready for our first dance, wifey?" I ask.

"I'm ready for you to hold me against your chest as you whisper dirty words in my ear to make me squirm."

"You know me so well."

Our song starts playing, and I take her hand and spin her so her back is tight against my body.

"Beckett? Did you—?"

"Learn how to dance? You wouldn't let me plan anything else. I thought I could at least learn how to dance in time for the wedding," I whisper in her ear.

Her eyes twinkle with happiness. I know I didn't have to, but seeing how happy she is, I'd learn every waltz, tango, and cha-cha. Hell, I'd learn to do ballet if I thought it would bring a smile to her face.

"Hold on tight, wifey," I say as I twirl us around the dance floor. I have to make a few adjustments to account for only having a left arm, but after the accident, I've learned how to do almost everything with one fully functioning arm and one residual limb. Odette was the first woman I dated who didn't look at me like I wasn't human, like I was broken. She only saw me—the man. A man she could fall in love with, not a man who needed fixing.

I squeeze her tight to my body and lift her off the ground. She squeals with happiness which almost bursts my heart open before I set her feet back down on the ground and continue the dance I learned. Even though Odette didn't learn the dance, she keeps up flawlessly. She used to dance as a child, and she knows how to read my mind, so it doesn't surprise me at all.

With every spin, my mind flashes with happy memories of us.

. . .

Our adorable meet-cute.

I step forward in line while staring at my phone. A huge mistake, I realize as burning hot coffee spills all over my hand and phone. I'm already in a foul mood, and this just made it a hundred times worse. I open my mouth to accuse the person who just spilled coffee all over me of not paying attention. An asshole move, I know.

Instead, my jaw drops to the floor when a woman, no, an angel stands in front of me. She has beaming eyes, a gorgeous smile, and waves of blonde curls. Her white sundress still looks flawless on her, even though it's now covered in stains.

I wince when I look up at her, realizing I'm the one who ruined her dress, but all I see is pure joy on her face, and I'm pretty sure a halo around her head—definitely an angel.

"I'm so sorry. I'm an asshole. I was looking at my phone instead of looking where I was going. Can I pay for your dry cleaning?"

She gives me a smug smile. "No."

"No?"

"You can buy me another cup of coffee and talk with me before you persuade me to give you my number."

A shit-eating grin spreads across my face. I think I'm in love.

We spent hours in that coffee shop ignoring everyone else. She canceled a dinner with her brother, while I failed in killing my target.

The first time I told her I loved her flashes next.

· · ·

"Do you want to come up to my apartment?" Odette asks, as I lean back from our kiss.

Hell yes, I want to come up to her apartment. I've wanted nothing else since I picked her up at her classroom. She teaches kindergarten and stayed late turning the room into a winter wonderland for the kids the next day. I haven't been able to keep my eyes off her ass even though her clothes weren't all that tight—a knee-length gray skirt and maroon sweater. She looked gorgeous for our first date without even trying. And if I come up to her apartment, I'm not going to have any control around her.

She laughs, reading my mind. How does she do that?

"Come on." She doesn't take no for an answer.

I follow her up, putting my hand in my pocket to keep from touching her. Stay in control.

She opens the door of her small loft, revealing a living room crammed full of plants, books, and crafts.

"You can come in; I don't bite."

I laugh. It's not you that I'm worried about.

I step into her apartment. She stands on her tiptoes and kisses me. A kiss I feel fucking everywhere. And when she pulls away, I do something worse than fuck her on the first date.

"I love you."

I wait for her reaction. For her to freak out. To kick me out. To say I'm crazy. Instead, she kisses me back. "I can't wait to fall in love with you, too."

Four months later when she finally said it back.

.   .   .

I'm balls deep in her. Her body is clenched around me. Her hands are on my shoulders as she bounces up and down on my dick.

"Are you close?"

"So fucking close."

I grab her ponytail, knowing my girl likes it a bit rough just before she comes.

"I love you," she screams.

I stop, not believing she just said that.

"Don't fucking stop!"

I chuckle and kiss her before I let her come on my cock.

After we recovered, she said she loved me with tears in her eyes. Every happy moment with her flashes like lightning through my brain. There is too much happiness to process it all.

I fell instantly in love—with her laugh, her brightness, her kindness, her independence. She doesn't rely on her family for income or a job. She doesn't need expensive things. She doesn't live in fear of the danger lurking around every corner. And most of all—she isn't a princess in need of saving.

Odette Monroe is normal. She lived a perfectly happy life without all the death and loss that existed in my world. And I instantly wanted to be a part of her life.

So that day, I made a choice to give up my life of crime. I stopped working for my half-brother and his wife. I gave up my friends. I gave up my nieces and nephews. I gave up everything to start over again. I found a new job in marketing that pays well enough, I moved into Odette's tiny loft with her, and I've never looked back.

I keep my past and present separate to keep my wife

and future family safe. I know how much my brother and his friends struggled and still struggle to keep their families safe. Every day is a fight to keep their enemies away. I don't want that for my family. Sure, it's tough rarely seeing them and only under careful secrecy. It was tough not inviting them to the wedding and only seeing my nieces and nephews once or twice a year, but it's necessary. I'll do everything I can to keep Odette and my future children, that I plan on having with Odette very soon, safe.

When I started dating Odette, I didn't think a woman like her, such an angel, could ever love a man like me. A man with blood on his hands. A man who is surely going to hell for all the sins I've committed. But on one drunken night after a month of dating, I finally told her the truth. I told her exactly who I am—a criminal, a weapons dealer, a drug dealer, a thief, a torturer, a murderer.

She said it didn't matter about my past, only about my future. That was the night I knew for sure I was in love with her and that I would do anything for her, including giving everything up. A year later, here I am, married to the most incredibly perfect woman. An angel I can only hope to be as sweet and kind as. A woman I get to love for the rest of my life. I can't think of a better way to spend it.

My two worlds can't cross. I won't put her or our future family in danger. It means seeing my brother and friends less. It means giving up everything before her, but Odette is worth it. I won't lose her.

Something won't let me forget that girl who interrupted the ceremony, though. An unnerving feeling makes me think danger is closer than I realize.

I shake the feelings off. Old habits die hard. That's all this is. I can't stop seeing danger when there isn't any. So I let the uneasy feelings go, despite my gut saying otherwise.

———

We step off the elevator on the top floor of our hotel hand in hand. Odette laughs at a stupid joke I made. Her laugh is infectious. It's the most beautiful thing I've ever heard, and her smile the most gorgeous thing I've ever seen. Same goes for her blue eyes, blonde hair, and curves. I love everything about her.

We reach the door of our suite before I stop. There are limitations to only having one arm, but this won't be one of them.

"What are you doing?" she squeals as I wrap my arm under her ass, lifting her into the air. Her legs wrap around my waist while her arms cling to my neck.

"Carrying you into our honeymoon suite." It may not be honeymoon style, but it doesn't matter.

She giggles, slightly tipsy from the champagne we were drinking at the reception.

"You don't have to—"

I kiss her lips. "I want everything to be perfect for you, today and every day."

"Okay," she says, her eyes growing darker as I carry her over the threshold. Her eyes are still on me as we enter the room.

I nod for her to take a look at her surroundings.

Slowly, she peels her eyes off of me and looks around the room. "Oh my god, Beckett, this is too much! You shouldn't have—"

I capture her lips with mine, so she stops saying things about how expensive the room is or that we can't afford it.

I want to give her the world. Tonight is nothing compared to what I have planned on our honeymoon. I want to spend every penny I earned through less than moral means on her—my way of making amends to the world for my sins.

She moans against my lips, completely forgetting about the expensive suite.

I've been in control all day. I didn't fuck her in the bathroom even though I knew she would have if I'd asked her. But now that we are alone together, I lose all control. I grind against her as I hold her up. I don't want to fuck her up against the wall. At least, not the first time I fuck her as husband and wife; that will come later.

I carry her to the bedroom, and we fall together onto the bed. We devour each other. Our tongues tangle, our moans sync, our hearts beat as one. We were so made for each other. My hand roams over her body, feeling the mix of fabrics beneath my fingertips. I want to rip the dress from her body, but I'm not sure if she wants to save the dress as a keepsake.

I'm about to ask her when she sits up suddenly.

"Shit, I forgot to take my insulin at dinner."

Odette has type one diabetes, and I know how important it is that she takes her meds on time.

I inwardly curse that I'm going to have to peel myself off her for even a second to go retrieve her bag, but it's for the best. We have all night together. Our flight tomorrow isn't until the afternoon, and I plan on enjoying every second we have together until then.

"It's been less than two hours since we had dinner. You should be good. I'll get them from your bag," I say, climbing off the bed in search of our bags. We ended up having dinner much later than everyone else since Odette couldn't get enough of my new dance skills.

I search the bedroom, closet, and living space, but I don't find our bags. I pick up the phone and dial the front desk, assuming our bags are still with the bellhop, but there's no answer.

I sigh, running my hand through my hair.

I loosen my tie and toss it aside, as well as my tux jacket, knowing what I need to do next.

"I have to go downstairs to get the bags. The front desk isn't picking up. Do you need anything else while I'm down there?"

She leans up on her elbows, staring at me with such heat in her eyes that I almost say fuck it, I'll get her insulin after. But I know that will be a mistake when her blood sugar spikes or drops and we spend the rest of the evening with her sick. I love her too much to hurt her.

So I talk my cock down. *Soon, buddy, real fucking soon.*

"Just for you to hurry back." Her hand trails down her cleavage.

I gulp as my cock hardens in my pants. There is no way I'm going to be able to walk with this hard-on.

Jesus, she's making my job difficult.

"Don't move. Don't undress. I'll be right back."

She laughs at my strained words as I run out of the bedroom. I press the button on the elevator a thousand times like that is somehow going to make it arrive faster. I adjust my cock discreetly, getting my bulge to decrease enough to not make a scene when I arrive in the lobby.

I step on and press the ground floor button repeatedly on the way down, begging the elevator to move faster. The doors open on the second floor, and I immediately hit the closed door button as an elderly man tries to step on.

Sorry, old man, you can take the next one. I have a hot as sin wife lying in my bed waiting for me. You understand.

After chewing the front desk worker's ear off for not sending the bags up and not answering the phone when I called, I am promised that the bellhop will be bringing the bags up immediately along with a free bottle of wine.

I jog back to the elevator banks and once again press the button repeatedly.

Come on, come on, come on.

The bell chimes as the elevator doors open.

I move to step on but stop in my tracks.

A woman rushes off, colliding into me.

I grab her shoulder, steadying her.

It's the same woman from before with the raven hair that interrupted our ceremony.

Our eyes meet.

This time the fear from earlier that I was expecting is there.

But just as I notice her anxiety, she blinks it away like I fucking imagined it. She shudders out of my grasp.

"Excuse me," she says as she flees.

So strange.

I move to step onto the elevator when I look down at my hand.

It's covered in blood.

What the hell?

I glance at the woman just as she exits through the revolving door. I get one last look at her and realize she's covered in blood.

I squeeze my eyes shut, silently cursing myself for what I'm about to do. I want nothing more than to step onto the elevator and go back to my wife, but something about the woman unnerves me. Whoever is chasing her could be a danger to my new family.

It can't be a coincidence that I saw the woman twice now.

I have to find out who she is and get her to talk to me so I can protect Odette.

It will take twenty minutes at most for me to get her to talk, get her in an ambulance, and call up reinforcements if I need help keeping Odette safe.

Twenty minutes until I'm back with my wife.

I run out the door of the hotel and hope like hell that I don't regret it.

2

RI

When people are faced with fear, they do one of four things: freeze, fawn, fight, or flight.

I've done the freeze thing. It didn't keep me safe.

I've tried the fighting thing. I lost. I have the bruises to prove it.

Fawning only made me sick to my stomach every time I agreed to a request.

My only option left is flight.

So that's why I'm running.

I have no choice.

The only way this plan will work is to keep running, keep moving, don't stop.

Clearly, I haven't thought my plan through. I can't always be running, but I don't have time to stop and think about how stupid my plan is. I have to keep running.

I could hide?

The idea creeps in as I run through the streets of Chicago.

Hiding will only be temporary.

Run first, hide later.

That's my new plan.

Run, hide. Run, hide. Repeat, forever.

It's not a good plan, but it's all I've got.

I don't feel anything as I run. My body feels like it's floating on air with every step. My brain tries to process what happened, but there is a haze, a fogginess. I let the haze cover the truth. I'm not ready to face it. Not today. Not ever.

Another survival technique I learned from an early age is to push down secrets. Hide them. Don't let them out. Don't think about what just happened. Then you never have to face it.

I'm good at it.

It's how I've survived this long.

I still can't believe it came to this. I should be going to sleep so I can wake up, go to classes tomorrow, and then go to my waitressing job in the evening. I shouldn't be here, running.

I want to turn around and see if I'm being followed, but it would slow me down, and I can't spare a second. If I do, the darkness will find me. I feel the dark wave growing speed and getting closer.

And then, I hear footsteps.

They're getting closer.

I chance a look, just a quick one, ensuring my feet keep flying forward.

Smack.

My head bounces off something hard. My legs are forced to stop even though they are itching to move again.

I realize I've hit a hard chest. I wasn't looking where I was going, so I probably stumbled into someone.

"Sorry, excuse me," I say, moving to run around the man whose chest I ran into.

A hand tightens around the back of my bicep.

My eyes close, my heart squeezes, my world stops. I've been caught.

I didn't even make it a whole day.

Finally, I look up, ready to face my captor. I've lost, and fighting will only bring more pain. But the eyes I look into aren't those of the devil I've been running from. These eyes are a sharp, steely chestnut brown. Dangerous eyes that tell me he could end my life with one squeeze of his hand. And yet, something fluttering in my chest tells me he won't.

"You," I say accusingly.

He doesn't say anything at first, just stares me down like I just killed his goldfish. I haven't done anything to this man, though. I don't even know who he is, apart from when I ran through his wedding ceremony earlier. I don't have a clue why he followed me, but I'm not going to stick around to find out. He's wasting precious time I don't have.

"Let me go," I say, trying to wiggle out of his grasp as I beat on his chest.

He doesn't flinch at my punches. And he doesn't loosen his grip on my arm.

"Who are you?" he asks.

"I'm no one. Now, let me go!"

I beat against his chest again, but the man is made of steel or something. He doesn't budge.

"You're not no one. I'm not going to ask nicely again. Who are you? Who sent you?"

"It doesn't matter who I am. Let me go!"

I dig my nails into his arm until I'm sure I'm drawing

blood. He still doesn't let me go. He doesn't react at all except for a slight flare of his nostrils.

This man has experienced pain. Inflicting a little pain won't get me what I want.

I look him over. The most notable thing about him is that he's missing his right arm. My guess is he lost it in an accident or fight. He wasn't born this way. That's the pain he carries with him every day, but it doesn't hold him back. I'm just as trapped as I would be with any man.

I scan him top to bottom. His golden-brown layered undercut is more tousled than before. I'm sure his new bride is to blame for that, along with the missing tie, undone top buttons on his shirt, and jacket missing. He's an athletic man, lean and tall, but not too bulky. I would love to see what is underneath his clothes, but my eyes drift back to his face. Stern anger burns in his eyes. His tightened jaw is covered in a five o'clock shadow.

He's handsome. His bride is a lucky woman.

I glance behind me as his suffocating grip on my bicep tightens, almost cutting off the blood flow. He's strong. *But is he strong enough to fight the man I'm running from? And would he fight even if he was stronger?* I doubt it. He'd probably toss me into the fire without a second thought about how he'd be ending my life.

He shakes me, drawing my attention back to him.

"Who are you running from?" He changes his question.

"Why are you here? Shouldn't you be with your *wife*?"

"Not when her life is in danger."

"What? She's in danger?"

"*You're* the danger. You interrupted my wedding. You showed up covered in blood at my hotel. That wasn't a coincidence, not given my past. Now answer me. Who. Are. You?"

Who is this man?

I glance at the ring finger on his hand. "Seems like you got married just fine by the look of the ring on your finger."

"I'll torture you. I will do anything to keep my wife safe."

His breath is hot on my face, and I have no doubt that he'll follow through on his threat.

"So torture me."

His nostrils flare—his face inches toward mine. I flinch, expecting pain. My eyes squeeze, but when nothing other than the force of his hand still on my bicep comes, I open them hesitantly.

"Are you hurt?"

I blink rapidly. *Did he just ask me if I'm hurt?*

His eyes roam up and down my body, looking for the source of the blood.

"I'm fine."

"Don't lie to me."

"I'm not."

He tilts his head, getting a better look at my side.

I jerk my hand across my broken ribs. "Like I said, I'm fine. Nothing I can't handle."

His gaze softens.

I bite my lip, trying to keep any unchecked feelings from creeping up. This man is far too attractive for a sinister criminal. He's way too comfortable corning me in a dark alleyway and threatening to torture me. This isn't his first time.

I can't want him. He's a monster, not to mention

married. *Don't let the hint of kindness in his eyes affect you. He'll ruin you the first chance he gets.*

But then his hand releases my bicep and inspects the wound on my side. And damn, does his touch warm my cold heart to him. Until...

"Hey, that hurts," I hiss and jerk back into the brick wall of the building.

"You should see a doctor. You're going to need stitches. The cut is deep, but it didn't hit any major organs. If you don't get stitches, it will get infected and leave a bad scar. And if you don't stop the bleeding, you'll die."

"I know what will happen! Do you really think this is the first time something like this has happened to me?"

"I'll call an ambulance for you."

"I don't need an ambulance."

"You're going to walk the twenty blocks to the hospital in your state?"

"Well, no, but..." I was hoping since he's already so invested that this guy would do me the honors of taking me. *But then why would he?* It's clear he hates me. And it's not like he has a car handy. Men like him, though—powerful, rich men, always have a way of using money to help them.

"What's your name?" His tone is softer, kinder this time. It seems since he didn't get me to answer with threats that he's going to try the honey approach.

"Why do you want to know my name? Just kill me if you think I'm a threat." I think that through a minute. "Actually, yes, kill me. I don't want to spend my life running. And any threat your family faces will die with me. They aren't after you; they are after me."

"Tell me your name."

"Tell me yours."

"Beckett."

"Beckett what?"

"Just Beckett. It's technically my last name, but I don't like my first name. I've always gone by Beckett. Maybe I'll take my wife's last name, Monroe, now that we're married."

"How very modern of you."

"Name," he says sternly.

"Ri." I expect him to ask my last name or my full name, something more than the short nickname I go by.

"Thank you for telling me, Ri."

My lips twitch up into something that resembles a smile. *Why am I smiling at this asshole? He's still holding me hostage in this alleyway when I should be running.*

He pulls out his phone from his back pocket and texts something.

I should run, but there is something drawing me to him. I don't know why but I feel safe with this man. He may be the devil, but maybe that's exactly what I need to keep the monsters from finding me—a devil on my side.

"Now, I can call an ambulance, but doctors will ask questions. Do you want that?"

"I thought you said I should see a doctor—that I don't have a choice?"

"You always have a choice. Go to the hospital, answer questions, and possibly end up in jail for your trouble."

"Why would I end up in jail?"

"Because you walked out of an elevator with blood on your hands. I'm sure the security cameras captured that."

"That's because I'm bleeding, you asshole!"

"Yes, but not all of that blood is yours, is it?"

My mouth drops. *He's good.*

"That's what I thought. Or you can walk away and take

your chances that the blood loss or infection won't kill you and that you'll only scar."

I frown and fold my arms over my chest. "Those are my only two choices?"

"From what I can tell, yes."

"What about you?"

"What about me?"

"You're not going to help me? Or get rid of me? You're just going to let me walk away? I thought you wanted to know who I was and how I put your family in jeopardy."

He smirks. "I got your name."

"You think Ri is my full name?"

"No, but it's enough."

"Enough for what?"

"To figure out exactly who you are and who is after you."

"Okay...but that still leaves me free."

"You're not a threat." He looks bored. "So what will it be? Do you want me to call that ambulance for you?"

"No, jackass. I can take care of myself."

I shoulder past him, letting my hand linger on his chest to ensure I get the most amount of blood on him and to double-check my suspicions that he's packing as much muscle under his shirt as I thought. From what I can tell, he's extremely ripped.

I peek my head out once I reach the street. The road is eerily quiet, but I don't have a choice but to head out into it. There is no other exit except back to Beckett. *Some hero he is.* He's not even a good devil. He should have killed me. Despite my thin frame, lack of muscles, or knowledge of how to use a weapon, I'm more dangerous than I seem. And if they associated me with him, I'm now a risk to him.

I start running again, pushing the asshole out of my

head. I make it ten steps before I feel someone's strong grip on me.

For a split second, I grin. *Maybe he is my hero after all?*

But when I look up, it's not Beckett gripping my arm. And unlike Beckett, this man doesn't have a kind bone in his body.

3

———

BECKETT

I GET the weirdest feeling in my gut as I watch Ri walk away. Run is more like it. I've seen a lot of strong, badass women in my life, but never one that had such control over her fear. Whatever she's been through, life dealt her a bad hand.

Too bad I'm too much of an asshole to get involved. It's my wedding night, and I'm not going to bring whatever shit she's dealing with into my marriage. I don't know if she's a risk to my wife's life or not, but I'm not taking any chances.

Me: Do you need anything else on the girl?

Langston: No, I should be able to figure out who she is within the hour. The security footage from the hotel will make it easy to identify her.

Me: Text me when you do.

I can always count on my old friend to hack into security systems and figure out who people are. Langston is the best at it. He has her picture and the start of her name; it wouldn't shock me if he identified her within the next five minutes; that's how good he is.

I'm about to pocket my phone when I get another text.

Angel: This dress is itchy. I don't think I can last much longer...

Me: Wait five minutes! I want to undress you. Don't you dare start without me!

I run to the street from the alleyway. I look left toward the direction Ri went expecting to see the backside of her as she continues to run away. Instead, nothing.

I frown.

She couldn't have possibly run the full block before I looked for her. *Did she dart into one of the buildings?* They all look deserted.

It's like she vanished into thin air, like she didn't really exist at all.

The old me wants to go investigate. The intrigue almost gets to me when...

Angel: Oops, it just slipped off.

Her text is accompanied by a very naked picture of her lying on the hotel bed.

I groan.

Me: Oops, my ass. I'm going to make you pay for that.

I look left one more time, but it's clear which direction I'm going to be running toward tonight—my wife.

4

RI

MY HEART POUNDS as two sets of hands grab onto my biceps. My right arm is still throbbing from where Beckett seized me just moments before. These two men are brutes; my only way of escaping is to outsmart them.

I open my mouth to yell, even though I don't know what good it will do me. I doubt Beckett will come running to my rescue, and no one else is on the street. But before I can get a sound out, a hand clamps over my mouth.

I scream into his hand, but my muted wail barely carries beyond myself. I try biting, but this man is at least smart enough to avoid that. He holds my chin up, forcing my mouth to stay closed.

The two men start dragging me as I kick, trying to get free.

My only solace is these men aren't the darkness I was running from. This is just plain bad luck.

It means I could escape.

I'm shoved into the back of a van parked on the side of the road. The second all three of us are inside, the van

35

starts moving. There must be a third man in the driver's seat.

I struggle against their tight grips, but then my arms are jerked behind my back, and I feel the familiar thread of rope being tied around my wrists.

The hand moves from my mouth.

I instantly scream, which only makes it easier for a gag to be inserted.

Finally, I'm shoved hard to the floor. I land on my right side, directly on my open wound.

I groan at the impact and feel my skin burning. I'm guessing my cut has widened. Before this, I might have had a fifty-fifty chance at surviving without seeing a doctor. But now, I'm guessing my odds are more like thirty-seventy.

The two men are behind me, so I flip them off with my bound hands. Not that they notice, but it makes me feel better to do something.

I blink back the stinging tears, refusing to let them out.

They aren't the darkness.

The danger isn't that bad.

I've seen worse.

I can survive this kidnapping. And if not, death would be preferable to what awaits me if he catches me.

My eyes cut behind me, but the two men sit silently on the floor of the van.

The rope isn't cutting into my wrists, so I'm sure I could free myself if I really tried, *but then what?* There are still two huge men in the back of the van with me. I wouldn't make it far.

The van stops less than five minutes later.

The two guys immediately open the back doors and start dragging me out. My skin scrapes across the van's rough carpet. *Why not add a carpet burn to my list of injuries?*

They yank me to my feet, once again holding my biceps. They don't draw their weapons, nor do they speak —to me or each other. No words have been exchanged since they kidnapped me.

I wish they would speak; maybe then it would give me some clue as to who they are and what I'm dealing with.

They lead me into the back entrance of a building. It's only then do I hear murmurs of voices trailing down the hallway toward us.

I stop, but the man to my left yanks on my bicep, ensuring I move forward toward the voices.

Keep moving forward; it's better than the alternative.

We approach a door, and the men don't have to open it for me to know it's a nightclub. The boom of the base through the door gives away our surroundings.

We walk into the nightclub in a single file, but neither man lets go of either of my biceps as we head to the back of the room. The lights are dimmed and the club lights from the various discos and contraptions overhead flash so quickly that it's hard to make out much of my environment.

I already know not to hang my hopes on any of these drunk assholes in this club, but I don't expect such blatant ignorance. Eyes divert away from me if they notice the ropes, blood covering my torso, and my two captors. However, most of the people we brush past in the overcrowded club are too self-consumed to even glance our way.

We stop when we reach the corner of the club where there is a man dressed in all black standing in front of a rope that leads upstairs—no doubt to the VIP area. He glances quickly at the two men holding onto me with a slight raise of his eyebrow before he nods, then unhooks the rope, removing it from our path.

The men still haven't spoken as I'm simultaneously pulled and pushed up the stairs. The music quiets with each step up away from the main club area, but that only allows for more room for my heart to beat louder than the base.

"Who are you taking me to?" I ask, hoping they will give me some information about my fate.

As expected, they ignore me.

We reach the top of the staircase; the floor opens up to a vast area with clear views of the entertainment below. There are men lounging on couches throughout the fancier, less crowded version of what we just walked through. There are a few half-naked women sitting on a few of the men's laps, but otherwise, you might not think anything nefarious is going on up here.

I feel the danger the second I step foot inside.

The men immediately stop talking as soon as they spot us. Almost a dozen eyes land on me, and I wait for some clue as to who they are or what they are going to do with me.

Instead, I'm met with more silence. That's my first clue who they are. The second is a tattoo of a ghost on one of the men's hands.

"You're the Phantom Brotherhood."

"And you're smarter than you look," a man on the far end of the velvet couch says. He has an amber drink in his hand, and his legs are spread wide, taking up most of the couch like he doesn't give a damn that he's supposed to be sharing it with anyone else. He must be their leader.

His devilish green eyes turn toward the man holding

onto my right bicep, and I get a flash of the ghost tattoo on his neck. "Good job with this one. She'll go for a pretty price once we get her stitched up. Where'd you find her?"

"Wandering alone on State Street."

The Phantom leader's light eyebrows shoot up, and he cocks his head as a sly smile spreads over his face. "You are a brave one."

"Let me go or you'll be sorry."

"What is a pretty thing like you going to do about it?" He looks almost bored. His eyes only glistened when he saw dollar signs. He doesn't realize the truth—who I really am, how valuable I am, how dangerous I am.

"It's not me you should be worried about."

"Do you know who I am?"

"The leader of the Phantom Brotherhood."

"I'm Ares. I'm not afraid of anyone. I rule this club, these streets, this city. It's you who should be afraid of me."

I smirk. "I'm not afraid of you."

His nostrils flare. "Maybe I should enjoy you first before I sell you, see if I can change your mind."

I take a slow, steadying breath. My mouth is always getting me into trouble. I should learn from these men and stay silent more.

He chuckles. "What's your name, brave one?"

"Ri."

There's an audible gasp around the room. I feel everyone's burning stares—none more than Ares. His mouth falls open.

They can't know who I am, can they? I just said my nickname, not my full name.

Ares stands and walks over to me. The men on either side of me stare at me incredulously. I feel their grips loosen instead of tighten—*they know.*

I straighten my shoulders, trying to appear brave. I can handle these men. I just can't be returned to my life before. I'll do anything but that.

"How?" Ares asks, his voice breaking.

I frown, not sure what he's asking.

"How...?" He clears his throat. "Where have you been? What happened to you, Rialta?" He looks at the gash on my side.

I suck in a breath.

And then Ares takes a step back, running his hand through his long, dirty blonde hair and pacing around the room. "We have Rialta Corsi, Princess of Chicago."

There is quiet muttering around the room.

Ares stops suddenly, his eyes jerking to me. I can't tell if it's fear or excitement that he has me—maybe a bit of both. "Jesus, I have a Corsi princess. I'm about to become the most powerful man in the country..."

"Or you're about to become a dead man. I'm not sure how you are going to be able to explain to my father that you tied me up and almost sold me."

Ares's face drains.

"I thought you weren't afraid of anyone. I thought you ruled this city." I laugh. "Who really rules the city? The Phantom Brotherhood controls from the Little Calumet river to Washington Park, but only at the direction of the Corsi Crime Family. You have no real power unless we grant it to you."

Ares is silent once again, as is the rest of the room. That doesn't mean communication isn't happening between them. I've heard about the Phantom Brother-hood. They operate like ghosts, silently sneaking in and out while committing crimes. That's their strength.

"Let me go and I won't tell my father about this. Let me go and I'll show you mercy."

The leer on Ares's face scares me, but I don't show it.

"Oh, I have a better idea."

Just don't return me to...

"What do you do when you can't defeat the devil? You marry the devil's daughter."

I gasp, not expecting that.

He laughs. "Now, who's speechless?"

"You—you can't marry me. I won't do it."

"You don't have a choice, Princess. I know your father. If I marry you, he'll have no choice but to honor it. Your traditions require it. You don't do divorce. You're required to remain a virgin until marriage. Your father was going to marry you off soon for an alliance, so that alliance will be with me."

"My father will kill you for this."

"He won't." Ares rubs a strand of my hair between his fingers like he already owns me.

"I'll never marry you."

"You will. In fact, your father will ensure it after I tell him about how you ran away, seduced me, and then fucked me. He'll welcome me with open arms after he realizes that I'm willing to marry his whore of a daughter."

"He'll never believe you."

"Oh? When did your father become a feminist? He always believes men over women, but you already know that. It's why you ran away."

My eyes flicker around the hungry eyes in the room on no longer panicked faces. They think Ares's plan will work. He's going to rape me and then convince the head of the Corsi Crime Family that I begged for it—that I wanted it.

I close my eyes, trying to find a way out, a way to save myself, but I don't see a way out. I pray to god to send a hero.

When I open my eyes a few seconds later, Beckett is standing at the top of the stairs.

5
———

BECKETT

RIALTA CORSI IS a pain in my ass.

I knew it the second she interrupted my wedding. But it became even more true the second Langston called me to tell me who Ri was—a mafia princess.

I had just started walking back to the hotel when he called. I stopped dead in my tracks.

Ri wasn't a nobody like she claimed. She's a freaking mafia princess. No, she is THE MAFIA PRINCESS! The Corsi Crime Family rules this city, state, and half the goddamn country. You don't run a criminal organization without the Corsi's taking their cut. Their leader is one of the most feared men I've ever heard of. You don't cross him.

Langston was able to locate her being pulled into a van via a street security camera. From there, he followed the van to the Phantom Brotherhood's club.

Now here I am, standing in their lair, so I can rescue the princess and return her to the king before he thinks I had something to do with her disappearance and kills my entire family as vengeance. I made sure that Odette's

43

medicine had been sent to her room, along with the fanciest bottle of champagne they had as an apology for spending more of our wedding night away from her. Even though I'm doing this to protect her, I know I'm going to be spending the rest of my night making up for failing her tonight.

Ri is standing in the center of the room, with her arms tied together behind her back, blood still dripping down her side. She doesn't seem to have any new injuries, *thank god,* although I'm going to have a hard time not killing her myself when we get out of this mess.

"Aw, Beckett, what brings you here? Sick of Odette already?" Ares says.

I want to defend my marriage, my wife, my life, but I'm not sure if that is the way to get through to these men, so I stay silent. Don't show your cards until you have to.

I've never met Ares before, but I was sent here by my former employer to kill him the day I met Odette. He was selling women, and I was supposed to stop him. The irony of my situation doesn't slip my mind. I thought I was saving Odette by getting out of my criminal past. If I had stayed until I finished my last job, then I might not be in this situation, and she wouldn't be in danger.

It doesn't shock me that he recognizes me. People seem to talk about men who only have one arm. I'm noticeable.

Ares is dangerous, but I know I can better him. I just have to be smart about it. I'm outnumbered. My reinforcements are hundreds of miles away. As much as I'd like to kill every man in this room, I know my limits. I won't win that fight.

So instead, I answer, "Maybe I am."

"Your reputation precedes you; I always knew you

were a womanizer. I knew you'd never settle down with just one bitch. You come here to borrow one of mine for a night out? Or do you prefer to buy?" His eyes glisten with excitement. He doesn't think I have it in me to purchase a woman. He's right, of course, but I know the way to get what I want is to pretend I'm just as cruel as they are.

I chuckle. "I'd love to peruse your catalog, but I came here for one specific woman." My eyes linger on Rialta.

"Oh, how rude of me." Ares walks over to Ri, grabs her bicep, and jerks her forward, so she's no longer guarded on either side by his men. "I didn't introduce you to Rialta Corsi, my fiancée."

I don't react externally, but inside I'm fuming. Not because I give a shit about who Ri marries, but because he's going to make this infinitely harder than it needs to be.

"For the last time, I'm not your fiancée. I'd rather die than marry you." Ri tries to wiggle out of his grasp, but his nails just dig into her skin through her shirt.

"It doesn't seem like you have a fiancée, Ares," I say.

Ri smiles.

Ares scoffs.

I quickly assess the situation and come up with a plan. "I know you think that by marrying Princess here that you're gaining an alliance with Corsi, but you're wrong."

"I'm not. Princess is my ticket to all the power. It's Corsi's weakness. He'll be forced to give me what I deserve."

"Stop calling me 'Princess,' both of you," Ri snaps.

We ignore her.

"Corsi won't give you any power."

"He will."

I shake my head. "He won't. Not after I show him a

video of two members of the Phantom Brotherhood kidnapping Princess off the street."

Ares's jaw ticks. He knows I've got him. He can't marry her and become a prince like he wants. Her father will rule their marriage invalid. That's assuming Ares can get Ri to marry him without the rope and threats, something I doubt he'll be able to accomplish.

Ri smirks, but her eyes study me cautiously. After our previous encounter, she knows I'm not on her side. If I'm here to rescue her, then it's because I have an ulterior motive.

"What do you want?" Ares asks.

"The same thing as you."

Ares chuckles. "No way. Your marriage tomorrow to Odette has been planned for too long. You won't back out of that agreement for another, even if your agreement with Corsi would be more valuable than marrying a Monroe. You're just going to give her back to Corsi, and even if you don't give him the tape of my men, he'll know I was involved. I'm a dead man if I give her to you. I won't allow that."

To protect Odette, we announced that our wedding would be tomorrow, not today. That's why he thinks I haven't married her yet. Although, I don't understand his comment about my agreement with the Monroes. The Monroe family is a modest one. Odette is a school teacher; her father is an engineer; her brother is a loan officer. I would have nothing to gain by marrying into their family.

Ri studies me closely. She could fuck this up if she tells him the truth, that she was at my wedding today. She knows I got married.

"Give Princess to me, and I'll ensure that Corsi doesn't know it was you who kidnapped her."

"You want her so you can marry her? So you can form an alliance with Corsi?"

Odette, forgive me. This is to save you.

"Yes. As you said, my alliance with the Corsi family is more lucrative than my alliance with the Monroe family."

"I won't marry you either, you asshole," Ri says.

Ares slaps his hand over her mouth. But from the muttered curse under his breath, she must have sunk her teeth into his hand.

My lips twinge upward. She's feisty. She's going to need that to survive in this world, but it's why I want out. Odette is kind, not feisty. Odette is strong but not fierce. Odette doesn't have a savage bone in her body like Ri does. It's the difference between being born into a loving family and being born into a vicious one.

"You want Princess. I want an alliance and a promotion in my status. When you marry Princess, you'll cement your place as a prince in the Corsi bloodline. You'll tie the Black Empire to the Corsi family. I'm assuming your plan was to bring the Retribution Kings along with you instead of snubbing them completely. I want that alliance.

"The Retribution Kings might think they have a monopoly on weapons sales in this town. I want that contract with the Corsi's instead. It will be the three of us, the Corsi family, the Black Empire, and the Phantom Brotherhood. All connected. All feared. All equally powerful."

I have no idea who the Retribution Kings are. And as far as the Black Empire goes, I've already left. Sure, they're my family, and I can always count on them, but I got out of that life. The only thing I want from Corsi is a promise he won't come after me or my wife.

"You give me Princess, and I'll ensure that when I

marry her, the Phantom Brotherhood is looked fondly upon."

I'm not a king like Ares or Corsi. I have no power to approve an alliance between the Black Empire and the Phantom Brotherhood; only Kai Black can do that. And I have no intention of trying to get Corsi and the Phantom Brotherhood into some sort of agreement either.

But the benefit of not being a king is that I don't have to be a man of my word. I have no one but my wife relying on me. Once I get Ri, I'll ensure her safe return to Corsi, and I'll tell him exactly what the Phantom Brotherhood did. Corsi will annihilate them, and I'll be able to return to my happy life.

"Done," Ares says.

I step forward to grab Ri and get us the hell out of here. I have a lot of groveling to do with Odette to make up for abandoning her on our wedding night.

I grab Ri's other arm, gently pulling her, but Ares doesn't relinquish his grasp on her.

"If you betray our agreement, I'll take the thing you love most from you. And you'll ensure that no one works with the Black Empire again. You'll make enemies not just from me but from everyone we are connected to. You may think that the Phantom Brotherhood rarely speaks, but your betrayal we will spread like wildfire."

That's why I'm going to ensure that Corsi kills you all before you can say a word to anyone.

I pull on Ri again. She takes a step toward me, but Ares still doesn't let go.

"One last thing." Ares nods to a man behind him who has his phone out and presses record. "Prove that you aren't loyal to Monroe. Prove that you are a soon-to-be Corsi prince."

I don't flinch. I would want the same if I was in his position.

Odette, I know what I'm about to do is fucking unforgivable, but I promise I'll spend the rest of my life trying to make it up to you.

And then I kiss Princess.

RI

WATCHING these two fuckers argue about who is going to get to marry me pisses me off. I'm not property they can sell or control! If I marry anyone, I'm the one who gets to decide who that is, not these monsters. I would never marry either of them—over my dead body and all that. One kidnapped me, and the other is already fucking married! These would be some of the last men on earth I'd ever marry.

I see a phone being lifted to record Beckett one second before his lips land on mine.

It's like the wind gets knocked out of my body as he devours my mouth. It's so unexpected, so wrong, controlling, manipulative.

He's a cheater.

He's doing it to save you.

No, there is something in it for him too.

I expect a quick peck that will be over within seconds, but this kiss isn't that. This kiss is full of possession—something I hate. I'm not an object.

But damn this kiss—it brings me back to life in a way I

didn't know a kiss could. Beckett's lips start pressed against mine, our mouths closed, our breaths even.

And then his tongue is at my seam, demanding I open for him. At first, I refuse on principle. I won't do anything he demands, only if he asks nicely.

His hand goes to my hip just below my gash and tugs me against his hard body. Our skin collides, and he feels like a fire raging against mine. I've never felt so hot; I'm burning for more of him.

My hands are still tied behind my back. As much as I want to pretend I'm in control, I'm not. Beckett has all the power here.

His hand slowly slides up my body, avoiding my wound, over the curve of my breast, and then he gropes me.

I should pull away. It's completely inappropriate, but my body won't allow me to. I'll condemn him for his touch after we get out of here, but that doesn't mean I won't enjoy this. My nipple hardens, begging for more. And I sizzle with a spark he lighted. If he were kissing me for any other reason than trying to get us both out of here alive, I'd be begging for more.

His tongue crashes between my lips, and this time I have no power left to deny him or myself.

I open my mouth and feel his wet tongue slide over mine. To anyone watching us, it might seem like I'm surrendering to him, but as his tongue slips over mine, I push back. He relents. Our tongues continue to dance, whispering empty promises to each other. Beckett's promises something about saving me. I promise something about letting him go and not dragging him into my own danger. Neither of us are going to be able to keep our promises.

He bruises my lips with his kisses, taking out his aggravation on my lips. My twisted soul loves it.

When Beckett finally stops his kiss, we stare intently at each other. Neither of us understands what just happened. It was meant to be an act. Beckett kissed me to get us out of here.

Instead, that kiss shattered hearts and worlds.

Mine.

Beckett's.

And Odette's.

And a truth is whispered in my soul—*he saved me.* I thought my life was over. I thought I'd always be running until I eventually grew tired and ended my life to stop the pain. His kiss made me want to live again.

My swollen lips tingle for him to kiss me again. While Beckett's eyes say how much he hates me for making him betray his wife.

His wife.

Beckett will never be mine. He's married. He has a wife. He loves her, not me.

He kissed me to save me. And, I'm guessing, to save her.

Ares laughs. "Maybe you are really more power-hungry than I thought. But I'm not sure a heavy make-out session is enough."

Beckett jerks me to his body, until my ass is pushed up against his groin, and his arm crosses in front of my breasts. "She's mine. I'm done sharing her with any of you."

Ares pouts. "What? We can't even get a peek at the goods?"

"Fuck off. Princess. Is. Mine."

Don't believe those words. They are lies. He belongs to Odette, not me.

My ovaries don't get the message, though, because they are now exploding with thoughts of being Beckett's and producing little baby Becketts.

Ares's hungry eyes go up and down my body. Beckett's hold tightens on me, and a low growl escapes his throat.

"You have one week to prove it. Marry her, arrange the new alliances. If you don't honor our agreement by then, Princess becomes fair game, and I'll be taking everyone you love from you."

Beckett doesn't answer; he just silently yanks me away from Ares, then down the stairs and back to the nightclub. I struggle to keep up with how fast he's moving through the club. I want to tell him to untie me, but I know he won't. He may have just saved me from Ares, but that doesn't make Beckett my hero. He took me to some end. And he won't untie me until he trades me away.

We step out of the club, and I can finally breathe again.

Beckett pulls a knife from his pocket, holds the blade in his mouth, and grabs my wrists, yanking my wrists toward him.

"What are you doing?"

"What does it look like I'm doing?

I frown. *Okay, then. Don't ask stupid questions. Got it.*

A few seconds later, the rope falls free of my wrists.

I pull my arms in front of my body. I grimace at how sore my shoulders feel from having my arms tied behind my back for so long. There are red bumps and superficial angry-looking cuts where the rope once sat.

Beckett wipes my blood off his hands on his pants and starts walking without a word.

For a second, I consider running again. But look where that got me.

Instead, I run the couple of feet to catch up to Beckett before falling in step next to him.

I open and close my mouth several times, trying to figure out what question to ask.

Why did you come back?

Why did you kiss me?

Why did you say you were going to marry me?

Are you going to return me to my father?

I don't ask any of them, though. Usually, I'm a chatterbox; my mouth is always getting me into trouble. But after that kiss, I'm on edge. I don't know how I feel or what to think.

"Thank you," Beckett says.

"Huh?"

"You should start with a thank you for saving your life."

"Uh...thank you?"

He shakes his head. "Are you asking it or saying it?"

"Saying it. Thank you for saving my life. I have no idea why you did it. Or what is going to happen next, but thank you."

A vein in his neck pops. I can see the rage burning just under the surface of his skin, threatening to explode. I don't know how he keeps it contained.

As we walk back to his hotel, Beckett takes out his phone and texts someone before pocketing it again. We walk in silence the rest of the way.

I know I should run again and form some sort of plan. Beckett is a dangerous man. I don't trust him. But he just saved my life, and I'm too curious to know more about him to run.

We step into the hotel lobby, and I'm still not sure what Beckett is going to do. I doubt he's going to take me upstairs to his honeymoon suite and introduce me to his wife. My unspoken question is answered immediately when a blonde god starts walking toward us.

My heart skips a beat watching the gorgeous man approach us. He's wearing a black tux with the tie hanging loosely around his neck. A strand falls from the faux mohawk he styled his dirty blonde hair in and dangles over his eyes. He blows it up before running his hand through it. He looks like a rockstar with his short sides, long hair on top, and a hint of tattoos beneath the collar of his shirt.

He has a concerned look on his face until he spots me. His eyes widen, and his mouth forms a 'wow,' but it's not audible. At first, I think the wow is because he finds me attractive, then I remember I'm covered in blood.

This must be the man Beckett texted.

"I'm Caius," the handsome god says, extending his hand to me.

"Ri." I take his hand. It's strong and warm, but I don't get the shockwaves like I do when I touch Beckett.

"Take her to your room. Don't let her out of your sight for a second. Not even for bathroom breaks. I'll explain more when I get back from apologizing to my wife about tonight. I'll be back in fifteen minutes."

Caius is silent as he studies Beckett like he thinks he's lost his mind. But he quickly shakes that thought away. "Of course, whatever you need."

Caius takes my hand, this time pulling me toward him. We all walk together toward the elevator banks. Beckett presses the button, and the doors open instantly. We all step on with Caius still holding my hand like he's afraid

I'll run away. But it's Beckett's hand on the small of my back that gets me to step onto the elevator.

Caius presses a button for the tenth floor, while Beckett presses one for the sixteenth.

The elevator stops on the tenth floor. It's time to get off, to go with Caius. But as nice as he seems, I don't know him. At first, I don't move, but Beckett's hand on my back again guides me forward to follow Caius off the elevator.

"I'll see you soon, Princess."

"Can't wait, Hero."

He glares at my nickname for him as the doors slide shut. It serves him right for calling me Princess.

Caius studies me in complete confusion. He's still gripping my hand firmly, not in an aggressive sort of way, but also not in an endearing way either.

"This way," he says.

I follow him down the hallway to the last door on the end. He pulls out a keycard and opens the door.

The room is a standard hotel room. It has a white bed, dark desk, a couple of lamps, and a door I assume leads to the bathroom. He lets go of my hand once I'm in the room. I can hear him locking the door behind me as I walk to the window that has a decent view of the city lights.

"Um...can I get you anything to eat or drink?"

I turn toward him. He's standing awkwardly at the foot of the bed like he's not sure what he's supposed to do with me. His hand is rubbing the back of his neck.

I shake my head.

He stares at me, taking me in like I'm the most magnificent thing he's ever seen. I guess the blood isn't that off-putting. This boy must not spend much time with the opposite sex if he finds me attractive. I'm a mess in ripped clothes, covered in blood, and rope rash on my wrists. I expect him to boss me around or treat me like his little sister like Beckett does. He doesn't. While Beckett is probably close to a decade older than me, Caius is young, early twenties. He's got a boyish charm about him, while Beckett is all man.

"So, you going to ask me what happened?"

He gives me a lopsided grin. "I'm sure it's an epic tale, but I wouldn't be a gentleman if I didn't offer you a hot shower, change of clothes, and medical treatment first."

"How chivalrous of you."

He shrugs with a hint of a blush on his cheeks. He walks over to his bag and starts pulling clothes out for me.

"I'm sure these will be too big on you, but it's better than being covered in blood." His eyes dip up and down my body. "Are you hurt anywhere?"

"Yes."

He turns back to his bag and starts digging in the bag for more gear. He turns back to me after finding a first aid kit.

"Whoa, what are you doing?" He tries to avert his eyes, but his large blue eyes are locked on my chest. I'm wearing nothing but a bra and panties, having removed my shirt and yoga pants.

"I'm obeying your boss, so I don't get a sweet boy like you into trouble."

He smirks. "You think I'm sweet?"

"The sweetest." My eyes catch a glance at the bulge in his pants. *Okay, so maybe he isn't that sweet, but he's kinder than Beckett. That's a start.*

He walks to the bathroom. I hear the sink running, and then he returns with a wet washcloth. He starts rubbing it across my shoulder and then to the swell of my breast.

"See? Sweet," I say.

He laughs deeply. "I have my hand on your breast. I'd call me a pervert, not sweet."

I shrug. "You're taking care of me and removing the blood. When you grew up like I did, your actions seem kind in comparison."

His eyes twinkle with pity for me.

"Don't—don't pity me."

He doesn't respond. He just moves the washcloth to my stomach.

I hiss.

He bends down to get a closer look. "Your ribs look bad. And there's a bad gash here." He looks at his first aid kit. "I don't have anything to fix your gash, and you need the good painkillers to stop it hurting every time you breathe."

I shake my head. "I'm fine. I'm not worried about the pain."

I move past him to grab the clothes.

He catches my wrist.

I hiss from the sting.

His eyes widen when he sees the rash from the rope.

"Sit."

His voice is a command, but it's also soft and caring.

Reluctantly, I sit on the edge of the bed.

He kneels in front of me and goes to work on my wrists. He smears some ointment on them before wrapping them in bandages.

My heart flutters in my chest at how gentle he's being. A man like him is exactly the kind of man I should want. Don't get me wrong, I'd fuck Caius in a heartbeat. He's hot as sin. But after my kiss with Beckett...*Jesus, stop living that fantasy! It's never going to happen. Beckett's married.*

Maybe I should fuck Caius and get any crazy ideas of Beckett out of my head. Even if he wasn't married, Beckett hates my guts for making him cheat on his wife.

When Caius is finished wrapping my wrists, he kisses the inside of my wrist.

My panties soak with that tender kiss.

Apparently, I'm into good guys just as much as I'm into bad guys.

I lean forward and catch his lips with mine, deciding carpe diem. I need to seize every moment I can.

He tastes like chocolate and wine. Even his kiss is sweet. For a second, I get lost in the kiss, but he's almost too gentle with his lips to demand my full attention, and my mind quickly starts comparing his kiss to Beckett's. This one is delicious and tingly, but it's doesn't have me all hot and bothered.

Suddenly, the door opens.

We both jerk our heads apart as we turn and stare at the door.

Beckett is standing in the doorway, looking white as a ghost. I expect him to have some irate reaction at seeing me almost naked with Caius between my legs with swollen lips from our kiss. I expect him to call me a whore or yell at Caius for falling for my dirty tricks to seduce him and get him on my side or something.

Beckett walks in almost like he doesn't even see us.

"Beck? What's wrong?" Caius asks as he slowly stands.

Beckett runs his hand down his face, and somehow that brings him back to life.

"Odette's gone."

BECKETT

I STOP JUST outside our honeymoon suite. My stomach is in knots, and I want to throw up. It's the only way to deal with my guilt and anxiety. I don't deserve any relief; I deserve every ounce of stress wreaking havoc in my stomach.

I know I'm doing what has to be done to protect Odette. If it weren't for my past, we wouldn't be in this mess. I would have already fucked her every way imaginable—on the bed, in the shower, against the wall. I'd already have her snuggled against my body, drifting in and out of sleep until we both recover enough to fuck again and again.

Knowing I did what I had to in order to protect Odette doesn't absolve my actions, though. But Odette will. She'll forgive me for everything.

Leaving her on our wedding night.

My past putting her in danger.

Even kissing another woman.

Yet, I'll never forgive myself.

I open the hotel room door as the thoughts of my kiss

with Ri bubble up like hot acid in my throat. I wish I could say the kiss was horrible, that it stirred nothing in me, and it meant nothing. I had to make the kiss look real, but it was more than that. It was more than how her lips felt against mine, how her tongue battled mine, her head slanted to deepen the kiss, her soft moans only audible to my ears, or the heat from her body as I held her tight against mine. Yes, all of that felt good. But there was something else...something I dare not name.

I have to name it, though. Odette deserves to know the truth.

"Odette?"

She doesn't answer me. I purse my lips as I breathe slowly, trying to settle my erratic heartbeat and look of sheer terror on my face, so I don't scare Odette when she sees me. We aren't out of danger yet, not until I return Ri to the mafia and ensure the Phantom Brotherhood is taken care of, but I took a large step toward protecting Odette tonight. And I won't rest until she's completely safe.

"Odette?" I try again as I walk into the bedroom where I left her.

The bed's empty.

My heartbeat speeds up as I throw the bathroom door open. "Odette?"

Empty.

My head scans the bedroom, and that's when I spot the trickle of blood on the stark white sheets.

Did her period start? Did she run out to get tampons?

Did she cut herself and run out to get bandaids?

Is the blood meaningless, and she just went down to the bar after getting tired of waiting on me?

I take in more of the scene as a million possibilities

filter through my head of how she could be safe. I don't let the other ones in, not yet. I'm not ready to face the possibility that she was taken.

And then I see the indisputable evidence as I walk around the bed.

More blood.

A puddle of blood on the floor.

My stomach heaves, threatening to vomit at the thought of my wife injured because I wasn't here to protect her.

I pull out my phone and dial a number with one press of a button.

"Beckett? Did you get the girl?" Langston answers.

"Yes, but Odette is missing."

There's a heavy pause. "I'll go through all the security feeds in the hotel and surrounding area. Siren is here. She'll let everyone know to head to Chicago immediately. We'll be there tonight. We'll find her."

I hang up, reserving any strength I have for later conversations.

I know I can count on my friends to help. I should have had them here. I thought I was protecting Odette by keeping them away, but it will take them hours to get here. That's time we don't have.

So much happened tonight that it can't all be a coincidence—Ri, the Phantom Brotherhood, the Corsi family. Somehow one of them is involved in this. Either the Phantom Brotherhood kidnapped her to ensure I stayed in line, the Corsi family did thinking I'd kidnapped their daughter, or whoever Ri was running from did. I know one thing—I need to talk to Ri.

I start running through the hotel room when I remember Ri's condition. I grab my first aid supplies and throw the bag's loop over my shoulder as I head to Caius's hotel room.

As the elevator descends to their floor, it hits me. Odette is gone, and I might not be able to get her back. She could be injured, raped, or dead by now. I failed her. If I get her back, she'll be changed. I've seen it before.

I've lost, even if I win her back.

All color drains from my face as the doors open. My chest seizes, and I feel a thousand pounds of pressure descend on my heart as I walk into the elevator.

After a short ride, I'm running on autopilot as I pick at Caius's room's lock. In my haze, that seems faster than knocking.

I see their shocked faces as I enter, but I can barely process what I'm seeing. I walk to the window.

"Beck? What's wrong?" Caius asks as he slowly stands from between Ri's legs.

I run my hand down my face, and the blood rushes back to my brain until I can articulate what needs to happen to save Odette.

"Odette's gone."

"What do you mean she's gone?" Caius asks.

"There was blood. Too much blood." I lock my emotions away as I speak. I need to think clearly if I have any chance of saving her. I can't think with my emotions, so I lock them up and swallow the key for a later time.

"Is she...?" Caius stutters.

"Is she dead? Probably," I say heartlessly.

Caius's mouth drops open, his eyes water as the shock of what I'm saying hits him. "But her body's not there? So she might be?"

I nod.

Ri is silent this entire time sitting on the edge of the

bed in nothing but her bra and underwear. I ignore her. I'll deal with her soon enough.

"Caius, listen to me. I need you to call everyone we know. Everyone who might have any ideas of who would want to hurt her. Call the police. And then start looking for her yourself."

He blinks, coming out of stupor. "Yes, I'll...wait, what are you going to do? Ri needs medical attention."

I unhook the bag I had the foresight to bring up. "I'll take care of Ri. I think she can help us find Odette. Then I'll help find her."

Caius runs to the door. Just before he walks out, I say, "We're going to find her. I won't stop until I find her."

I can see the tears welling in Caius's eyes. I'm not sure he's strong enough to make the necessary calls and start the search, but it's more necessary for me to talk to Ri than the police. The police won't find Odette, but Ri might have a clue as to where she is.

The door falls shut, and then I'm alone with Ri. She's still sitting in her underwear on the bed. She hasn't reached for the clothes to dress herself. Based on how I find her with Caius, she knows how to use her body to control men.

"I'm sorry about your wife."

Her words cut like stone through my heart.

"Don't act like you're surprised she's missing, Princess."

Her features narrow. "I should go. I need to see a doctor, and you need to find your wife."

She stands.

I catch her arm and jerk her to me. My hot breath burns against her skin, and I know my touch against her side is painful, but she doesn't react.

"Sit. Down."

I release her, and for once, she sits without fighting me.

"I wish I knew where your wife was or who took her. I really do." She squeezes her eyes shut.

I put my bag on the bed and unzip it, digging out the supplies I need as I kneel between her legs just like Caius was doing.

Her eyes fly open. "You're going to help me?"

"Yes, because after I ensure you don't bleed out in this hotel or die of an infection, you're going to tell me everything you know. And then I'm going to use you to get my wife back."

I expect her to argue, to fight. Whoever I trade her to to get Odette back won't treat Ri kindly. My guess is it was her father she was running from in the first place. She won't want to go back to him if he's the one who stole Odette. And if it was the Phantom Brotherhood, then they'll rape her, try to marry her off, or sell her. Her future isn't pretty.

I look up into her eyes, gauging her reaction. There's a tear rolling down her cheek.

She wipes it away quickly, almost like she's embarrassed. "I'll do whatever I can to help you get your wife back."

The tear wasn't for herself. It was for my wife.

But this woman has hardened my heart to her after what I had to do to save her. And I don't trust her.

"You're an excellent actress, Princess."

"You're going to save her, Hero. If you did all of that just to save me, someone you hate, I can't imagine the lengths you'll go to to save her."

I pull out some gauze to soak up enough of the blood so that I can go to work.

"Hold that there."

She holds the gauze, and I quickly look around the room, finding a bottle of tequila on the dresser.

I grab it and hand it to her. "Drink. I don't have any painkillers or lidocaine."

She shakes her head.

"I have to stitch up your wound. I know how to do it, but it's painful. Drink." I push the bottle at her again.

"I'd rather be sober for what comes next. I can handle it."

"I doubt that, Princess."

I kneel between her legs again as I pull the needle out of the bag. This would be a lot easier with two hands, which just means she's going to have to help me hold the wound closed.

I take her hand roughly and place her fingers on one side of the wound. Then I grab her other wrist just as roughly and place it on the other side. I expect her to wince at my touch. She doesn't. But being rough with her hand and wound isn't the same as a needle piercing her flesh over and over again.

I push her hands together, closing the wound.

"Hold your hands like that while I stitch the wound closed. Try not to cry out; I don't want the neighbors to call the police."

She huffs.

I doubt the princess has felt pain. She may have grown up in a dark world, but she had her father to protect her. Women in his family grow up with wealth. They are treated like shiny objects, possessions the men can control and parade around. It's not a good life, but at least it's not one where she has to worry about dying or being tortured, just her husband dying.

I jab the needle hard into her flesh, knowing I'd rather her give in now than halfway through. I want her to fear me. I want her a little tipsy. It will make interrogating her easier.

I wait for the hiss, wince, or curse word. All I hear, though, is the steady rise and fall of her chest. I ignore her ample cleavage in my face as I stab the needle through her skin again.

No reaction from her again. Her body doesn't even flinch away from me.

I frown. She can't have that high of a pain tolerance unless...

I examine her bare abdomen more closely. There is still some blood and bruises from however she got this gash but hidden beneath the dried blood are scars. There is one just under her bra on her ribs. Another angling downward on the lower half of her stomach, disappearing beneath her underwear.

"Something wrong? I don't feel you jabbing me anymore."

"So you *can* feel that?"

"Of course."

"You don't react to it, so I thought maybe you were already drunk or took pain pills."

She shakes her head, and her eyes glaze over as if she's replaying why she has such a high pain tolerance.

I should feel sorry for whatever atrocities she faced in her past, but I don't feel anything but anger. I quickly finish stitching her up, realizing physical torture isn't going to work on her to get my answers. If it wasn't for her, I would have been here to protect Odette.

"Well, you won't die from bleeding out." I put a piece of gauze over the wound.

"Thanks."

I grab the clothes from the bed and toss them at her as I stand up. "Get dressed."

She catches the clothes and doesn't argue as she puts them on. The clothes are much too big on her. The black sweatshirt hangs down to her knees like a dress, and the gray sweatpants fall off immediately after she pulls them up.

I sigh and rummage through Caius's open suitcase. I find a pair of boxers and toss them to her.

She pulls them up and rolls them several times, but it's enough to keep them up. When she pulls the sweatshirt down, it hides the boxers. At least I know she's not wearing only her tiny panties underneath.

"Now that you're decent, start talking."

She frowns. "What do you want to know?"

Where my fucking wife is! But I keep my anger in check. If I explode, she might not talk.

"Everything. Who you are running from? How you were hurt? Were you sent as a decoy for me to follow while your father kidnapped my wife?" *Kidnapped, not murdered.* I can't believe she's dead. I have to hold out hope.

Even as I think about that possibility, my body doesn't register it. All I feel is fury. I don't feel sadness or terror or loss or grief. If I did, I would be a sobbing mess on the floor. I'd be drowning in my tears and cries.

Ri's face scrunches as she thinks. There is a long pause before she opens her mouth. "I can't tell you."

"What do you mean you can't tell me?" *Maybe I'm going to have to torture her after all...*

She folds her arms over her chest and walks to the window, looking out into the dark night. You can't see any stars in the middle of the city, just a sea of blackness and city lights.

"It wouldn't be safe for you if I told you. But my problems have nothing to do with Odette. The people after me aren't after Odette."

"Is it your father?"

"My father isn't after Odette."

"Your father would do anything to get you back. If he thought I had you, he'd take what's mine to keep me in line and ensure your return."

"Then offer up a trade. But I don't think my father has Odette."

"It's either your father or the Phantom Brotherhood—one or the other. Either way, it has to do with you. It has to do with whoever hurt you, whoever you were running from!" I stomp toward her.

She doesn't cower. She lifts her chin as I grab her neck, threatening her as I press my body hard against hers. "Tell me who hurt you. Tell me what you were doing interrupting my wedding. Tell me why you were covered in blood on the elevator at the same time I just happened to be stepping on. Tell me why my wife is missing."

Her eyes flick back and forth, searching mine for something. If she's looking for my trust, she won't find it. I will gladly give her up, sell her, murder her if it would bring Odette back to me.

I close my hand around her neck, reducing the amount of oxygen she's getting to almost none. Her face starts turning blue, her eyes bulge a little, but once again, I find no fear.

"Start talking." I release my grip enough for her to suck in a deep breath.

"You're not a monster. You're my hero. And you'll be Odette's too. But I can't help you."

I'm going to kill her.

The door flings open and Caius steps in. He doesn't seem shocked to see me squeezing the life out of Ri. I file that away for later, because it doesn't make sense. *Why would he allow me near his sister if he thought I was a bad guy capable of torture?* Odette said she didn't tell anyone else about my past, but it seems like she might have.

"The police are here, but I don't think we are going to get much help. I called everyone to keep an eye out for Odette."

Caius looks nervous as hell. He runs his hands through his blonde faux mohawk, tousling it as he paces the room.

"What is it?" I bark, losing my patience.

"I think I know why Odette was taken."

"Elaborate."

"They didn't want you to become king."

"King of what?" I frown, having no idea what he's talking about.

"The Retribution Kings."

8

BECKETT

RETRIBUTION KINGS—THAT'S the same name Ares spoke of. I thought he was speaking nonsense, but now I'm swirling with thoughts of what the group is and how Caius is tied to it.

"Sit down, Beckett," he says.

I still have my hand around Ri's neck, and she studies me curiously. I have no doubt that she knows more about the Retribution Kings than I do. She grew up in this world. If what Ares said is true, then the Retribution Kings are a rival gang to the Corsi family.

Reluctantly, I let go of Ri's neck and sit on the edge of the bed. Ri takes a couple of deep breaths, her chest rising and falling calmly beneath Caius's sweatshirt.

He walks over to her and strokes her cheek. "You okay, babe?"

Babe? Really? Such a cliche. I know they kissed, but that doesn't mean he gets to go around calling her a term of endearment.

"I'm fine." She smiles brightly. "But if you call me babe

again, I'll punch you in the face so that disgustingly sweet term of endearment never leaves your mouth again."

Caius's face stares incredulously at Ri.

I huff once in a sort of chuckle. If she had said that under different circumstances, maybe I would have laughed, but not when I'm worried about Odette.

Caius notices. "You should sit, too." He looks to me. "Unless you don't want her to hear all this, but I'm pretty sure she already knows, being who she is."

I shake my head; it's fine if he speaks in front of her. It's not like we have much choice. We can't just let her head to the lobby and hang out by herself while we talk. She's our best chance of getting Odette back.

Caius picks up the bottle of whiskey and holds it out to me. "Maybe you should drink some of this first."

His eyes are wide and terrified.

I take a swig of the bottle as much for his benefit as mine, while he paces in front of Ri and I.

"Speak. Who are the Retribution Kings? And why would I become king of them?"

"The Retribution Kings are a centuries-old group who cares about one thing—retribution. We have no loyalty to anyone but those who have proven themselves worthy of the group, who have passed our tests. Together we ensure order among the gangs, elites, mafia. Any group can hire us to seek their revenge. We only accept a job that ensures justice. We are judge, jury, and executioner. We decide who should be punished and how. We—"

I know I should be listening closer, but all I hear is Ri say, "We?"

Caius's jaw ticks nervously. He raises his hand and brushes it through his hair as he looks at me with a flushed face. He quickly glances from me to Ri, but even Ri's eyes have darkened as she stares Caius down like what he's saying is poison.

"My family has belonged to the Retribution Kings for generations. It's one of the most common ways of joining the group. The other is—"

"Marriage."

He nods.

Jesus. I stand abruptly, my fist tightening as the vein in my head bulges. I can already guess much of what he's going to say next, but I need to hear it. So instead, I walk back to the window and stare out to avoid looking Caius in the eye and most likely killing him. I should have had more than a swig of the whiskey. Maybe the alcohol would have cooled the burning blood in my veins.

"Odette is our family's princess, just like Rialta is the Corsi princess. We try to keep the women in our family out of danger by keeping them from knowing much of what we do exactly, but Odette being the princess, had one very important role..." Caius stumbles over his next words. "To find a man who could follow in our father's footsteps and become king."

I study him out of the corner of my eye as I rest my forehead on my arm, gripping the top of the windowsill.

He sucks in a breath like he knows he's about to get punched. "We picked you."

His words rush together like he's trying to hide the truth of what he is admitting.

"*We?*" I pick up on that word again. I'm beginning to hate the word.

The door bursts open as if I just said the magic word they'd been waiting to hear. Gage, Hayes, and Lennox walk in—my three other groomsmen. It's not because I'm best friends with them, but because I thought they represented my new world. A world free of dangerous men. They grew up with Caius and Odette. I enjoyed drinking a beer and watching a game with them. I never suspected I was in the presence of men who were born killers just like me.

Although, now that I know, I replay every conversation and gathering I've ever shared with them. There were signs. Either I was oblivious, or I just didn't want to think that my future wife was tied up with this shit.

"You're all Retribution Kings?"

Three sets of heads nod.

Ri takes in each of them but remains silent, not drawing attention to herself. And yet, she's a magnet to every man in this suite. All of their eyes run up and down her body with hot lust and desire. She doesn't flinch away from the attention; she basks in it. Her eyes flirt with each of them, telling each of them how much she wants them. All three of the men are fit, too fit. It should have raised a red flag that all of Caius and Odette's friends were super in shape and weren't physical trainers, athletes, or models. I should have known they stayed in shape out of necessity, not vanity.

"Did you find her?" Caius asks.

Now they have my full attention. Of course, they've been out looking for their lost princess.

Their princess.

Odette was never mine.

She was always theirs.

It was all a lie.

But I still cling to every word. My feelings don't disappear just because I find out Odette lied to me.

"We haven't found her. Whoever took her wiped all the security feeds. I'm scanning the nearby security cameras, but they knew how to avoid being seen," Gage says as he sits down on the bed with his laptop going back to work. I assume he's the tech wizard of the group. He told me he was an accountant. He wears dark jeans and a leather jacket that looks sharp against his black skin as he sits on the edge of the bed.

"Gage will find her. Have you finished telling him?" Hayes asks Caius. He, too, is dressed in all black like he's ready for a fight. His long dark hair is pulled back in a man bun, and he wears full-frame glasses. He walks over and leans against the wall looking over Gage's shoulder.

I glare at Hayes. He told me he was a real estate agent.

"No, I haven't finished telling him everything," Caius says, annoyed with his friends.

"Well, get on with it. We should be searching for Odette, not listening to storytime," Lennox says. His reddish-brown hair is textured in a long French crop hairstyle. Tattoos riddle his body from head to toe, at least what I can see that's not covered in his long black sleeves. The liar told me he was a software engineer.

"You should be searching instead of listening," I snap.

"Is that an order, boss?" Lennox grins, knowing it's going to piss me off.

I don't want to be the leader. I wanted a quiet life with my wife, not trying to wrangle these guys who are still boys in every way. They think they are invincible, that they can rule the world. I know because I used to be just like them. And they won't learn until one of them ends up six feet underground.

"What leads do we have?" I ask, ignoring Lennox's taunt.

"Not much; we think whoever kidnapped Odette was trying to stop your wedding. They got the fake information we sent out that the wedding wasn't until tomorrow. They wanted to stop you from taking over," Gage says.

"Why would they care if it was me or someone else?"

Silence stretches around the room. "Because they know your past, same as us. You're the only man who can do this job," Caius says.

I frown, not understanding, but it doesn't seem important now. All I care about is finding Odette. Then I can come back and murder these bastards for lying to me and interfering with my life. I'll fight to the death to get her back, but I have to know what I'm fighting for.

"Was it all a lie? Or was it basically an arranged marriage? One you all forced on her?" I move from the window, staring each of them down in turn—Caius, Gage, Hayes, and Lennox.

All of them look anywhere but me. The only one meeting my gaze is Ri, the only person I don't want to be thinking about right now. There is sympathy floating out beneath her long eyelashes.

I glare back, wanting none of her sympathy. All I want is her hate, so that's all I'm going to give her back. I hate every person in this room for lying to me, for having a part in my wife's disappearance.

"You were Odette's mark when you met in the coffee shop. We had scouted you for months and finally saw a chance to draw you out to Chicago where you two could meet," Lennox says, not holding back. Apparently, he's the brave one.

My heart sinks.

"My sister cared about you, though. You may have

started off as basically an arranged marriage, one that would benefit her family, but the feelings she felt for you were real. She cared for you a lot; possibly even loved you. She'll tell you that."

My heart sinks. *Possibly? Odette possibly loves me? When my heart only beats because of her?*

"Who took her? You all have your suspicions. Who. Took. Odette?"

I scan the room. This time the men at least have the balls to look me in the eye. My anger bubbles through me, and if I don't have something to take my rage out on soon, I'm going to beat the shit out of all of them before I go find Odette myself.

"Either the Phantom Brotherhood or the Corsi Family," Hayes says, his eyes landing on Ri.

She squirms where she sits on the bed, looking uncomfortable for the first time to have all the attention on her. We are right back where we started, needing her to talk.

"So either the Phantom Brotherhood took Odette to ensure that I followed through and married Princess to ensure their alliance, or Corsi did to ensure I returned his daughter to him unharmed," I say.

Everyone nods and grunts in agreement.

I have to torture Ri to get the answers, but I want to know everyone's thoughts first.

"If your life was dependent on choosing who took Odette, who would you bet your life on?" I'm asking them to bet their life on this, because if we don't find Odette, I'm holding them all responsible.

I look to Caius first.

"Corsi," he says, his eyes flicking an apology to Ri.

I growl.

He snaps his attention back to me.

I turn to Lennox next. "The Phantoms."

"Same," Gage says.

"Corsi," Hayes says almost apologetically.

It's an even tie. Half the group thinks it was the Phantom Brotherhood, the other half Corsi. My gut doesn't have a strong inclination toward either of them. I'm still playing catchup, but I will soon.

"It's your turn, Princess. Who do you think took Odette?"

Her gaze locks with mine. I almost expect her to look to her new admirers for help. "I don't know, but I'm willing to do what I can to help."

I frown, my mind buzzing with the ways I plan on torturing it out of her.

The room is silent.

"Shit, we have to tell him," Hayes says, gathering his nerve.

"Tell me what?"

Hayes's eyes water, but he doesn't speak.

Gage keeps staring at his computer hiding behind the screen.

Lennox grabs the bottle of whiskey and drinks a long swig from it.

Caius's bottom lip quivers.

Princess walks cautiously to me. Her movements, above everyone else's, I don't understand. Everyone else is a coward, while she's the only one who will face me.

Gage clears his throat through a sob. "The blood—you saw it—there was too much—there is no way Odette survived it. All we can do now is get retribution for her."

My heart thumps to a stop, and then I fall, my grief and fear consuming me. I believe his words because my heart already knew what I was too afraid to admit out loud.

Odette's dead, and I'm not getting her back.

9

———

RI

BECKETT COLLAPSES as soon as Caius implies that Odette is dead. I reach out to hold him, and his body is heavy in my arms. I don't think he passed out, just disintegrated from his grief.

I wait for the tears, sobs, and screams that usually accompany grief, but Beckett does none of those things. That's not true of the rest of the room. Caius had been holding it together up to this point. Now, hot tears stream down his cheek as he cries out at the loss of his sister.

Lennox slides down the wall, his head falling into his hands.

Hayes grips Gage's shoulder tightly, like it's the only thing keeping him upright. Gage closes his eyes, turning it all inside until his fist slams down on the bed in rage.

All of the men in this room are some of the hottest I've ever seen. I wouldn't mind spending a night in bed with any one of them. But of course, my stupid heart has to want the man who's currently in my arms mourning the love of his life. Even if I got him into bed, I'd be nothing but a rebound.

Slowly, Beckett comes to his senses and rebalances himself as he moves out of my arms. He gives me a stern look but doesn't thank me for catching him, holding him, trying to comfort him.

His eyes look dead. Not angry, sad, or emotional—just blank.

He's in denial. The only way to protect himself is to focus on the tiny chance that Odette somehow survived. That she's not dead.

He can't accept her fate yet. And if I was Odette, I wouldn't want him to. That's how I know he loves her. She's his entire world. It only makes me want Beckett more. My heart aches to be loved as much as Beckett loves Odette. It's all I've ever wanted, but I won't act on my feelings. I won't ruin a love like that if there's a chance that Odette's alive.

I hear sniffling behind us. I don't know if it's coming from Caius or Lennox.

"I refuse to accept that Odette's dead until I see it with my own eyes. She's a fighter. She won't go easily," Beckett says.

Silence. It's clear the guys don't agree, but they aren't going to argue with Beckett now.

"So if I'm your king, then you have to do what I say?" Beckett tests them.

I don't know much about them, but I doubt even if they want Beckett to be their leader that it will be that easy.

The guys all look to Caius. My guess is he is used to being the leader of the group.

He lifts the hem of his shirt up to wipe his eyes, revealing row after row of hard abs. I feel myself drooling at the sight and try to reign myself in, but these guys are intoxicatingly sexy. If I ran into any one of them on the street, I'd be flirting like crazy with them. It's hard being surrounded by so many gods at once.

Beckett clears his throat next to me.

My eyes cut to him as he glares at me.

I don't know why he has a problem with me staring at Caius. It's not like Caius is in a place to fuck me either, having just lost his sister. Although, people grieve in different ways.

I really need to get my head out of the gutter.

"Not exactly. Technically, Dad is still the leader. He's been sick for a while, which is why Odette, um..." Caius stutters when Beckett shoots daggers at him with his eyes for talking about why Odette chose Beckett. He doesn't realize that he wouldn't have such strong feelings for Odette if it wasn't real love. She had to have loved him too.

"You have to complete initiation before you can have the full power of being leader," Lennox finishes for Caius.

Caius gives him a small nod for saving him from Beckett's murderous stare.

"You aren't the rest of the Retribution Kings. You all arranged for Odette to marry me because you wanted me to be your leader." Beckett spits out his words like he's disgusted by them. "Can I count on the four of you to accept me as your leader?"

"Yes," all four of them say at once.

Beckett turns to Hayes and Gage. "I want to know everything on the Phantom Brotherhood. I want eyes and ears on them. I want to know if they have Odette."

Surprisingly, Hayes and Gage nod and head out of the hotel room.

Beckett turns to Lennox next. "Same goes for the Corsi family. Take Caius and find out if they took her."

And then it's just me and Beckett left. We are standing no more than a foot away. I expect the interrogation to begin. He thinks I have information about where his wife is, even though I can't tell him any more than I already have. He'll kill to get Odette back. He'll kill me to save her.

"Your father is who you're running from, isn't it?"

"I don't know if my father took Odette or not."

"That's not what I asked. Are you running from your father?"

"He's a cruel man who wants to marry me off and has less than ideal beliefs about a woman's position in this world. Why wouldn't I run from him?"

"Who are you supposed to marry?"

I tilt my head, unsure why we are talking about the man my father arranged for me and how this fits into finding Odette.

"It doesn't matter. I didn't choose him."

He frowns as he sinks back onto the edge of the bed. That's when I realize why he's asking. He's trying to figure out how Odette felt being told that she needed to marry him.

"I'm sure it was different for Odette. She had time to grow into her love for you. And I'm sure Caius and the rest would have found someone else for her to marry if she didn't fall for you. She loved you." I sink next to him.

"You don't know that."

"How could she not, Hero? You saved her and fought for her. You're what every girl dreams of—a knight in shining armor."

He huffs. "Some hero I am. I couldn't even protect her after only being married a couple of hours."

We sit in uncomfortable silence. I'm not sure why he

isn't questioning me or going with one of the guys to search for Odette. Suddenly, a knock raps at the door.

"Come in," Beckett says.

The door opens, and people start piling in. I don't know how everyone seems to know how to pick a hotel room lock so easily.

"Tell me you found something. You saw her on the security cameras in the hotel or on the street. You have some clue where she is." Beckett's voice is dripping with fear. Before, he was hiding his emotions from the guys, trying to appear stronger than he is, but with these people, he shatters.

A woman walks over to him and wraps him in her arms.

He wraps his arm around her and hugs her back.

The blonde man looks down at them with sadness. "I'm sorry. Whoever took her knew what they were doing. I've looked through all the security footage within a three-block radius, and there's nothing. I'll keep looking beyond that, but I don't have a good feeling." He looks at me, like he wants to say more but won't with me in the room.

The taller man next to him with broad shoulders and long hair looks at me as well.

Then the woman does.

My eyes shoot to all of them. It's clear they know who I am even though I don't know who they are.

"Do you have any other leads?" the larger man asks.

"I sent half of the guys after the Phantom Brotherhood and the other half after the Corsi Family. Hopefully, they will turn up some sort of clue as to which group took her. I'm just not sure how skilled the boys are."

"Have you gotten anything from *her* yet?" the first man asks.

"No," Beckett answers.

"Wait. You mentioned others helping you? I thought everyone here were civilians?" the woman asks.

Beckett gently pushes her off his lap, and she takes her place next to the blonde man. He hangs his hand on his knee. "Apparently, Odette was heir to the Retribution Kings. Our marriage was arranged so I would become their leader."

"I've heard of the Retribution Kings. They're ruthless and damn good at what they do. I don't know how they make money, but they wield their power by inflicting the most pain possible and setting examples of people who cross them in the worst ways possible. You don't cross them and live to tell the tale," the blonde man says.

"What do I do? They want me to be their leader—"

"So you be their leader. You use them to find your wife, learn everything about them, then decide what you want to do. You wanted out, but instead, you found yourself deeper in the darkness," the woman says.

"But we can't stay if you work with them. I agree with Liesel; they are your best chance at finding your wife. They're skilled; they know this area; they know the players involved. And they won't take kindly to us being here. They will see us as their enemy and will think your loyalties are split between us and them. Make them believe you're loyal to them, and we'll do what we can from the shadows. After you find Odette, then you decide whose crew you want to be part of."

"I don't know how I'm going to do this without you guys by my side."

Liesel smiles. "Yes, you do. There's a reason you didn't want us at that wedding or in your life. You wanted a fresh start. We love you and will always be here for you, but now is your chance to find yourself."

Beckett nods and then stands. He takes a turn hugging each of them. "I'm glad you're here, even if we don't get to see each other much after tonight. Even if it means you will be helping me from afar, I appreciate knowing that I always have you guys no matter what."

"Of course we'll always be here for you, man," the larger man says.

Their gazes start shifting back toward me.

"We can make her talk," the larger man says.

"I don't need your help to get her to talk. Unfortunately, I can't torture her until I know who has Odette. If the Phantom Brotherhood does, then I can do whatever to Princess to get her to speak. But if her father has Odette, then I need to be more careful how I extract the information."

I have limited time before he tortures me. He doesn't realize that nothing he could do to me would be half as bad as the simplest option—sending me back to the man who hurt me.

———

We search night and day for three days straight. Beckett keeps me by his side, asking me questions and getting more and more frustrated when I don't answer.

We storm into Caius's apartment early in the morning on the third day. It's a large penthouse in the middle of the city overlooking the river. We walk into the dining room, where a long table sits. It's become the headquarters of operation find and save Odette. We've walked in countless times, and it's always the same.

Caius is sitting at the end with a large pot of coffee next to a computer screen. His eyes are bloodshot, his hair a mussed mess, his clothes are wrinkled, and I'm sure if we got close, he'd smell of sweat and body odor from not showering for three days. It's pretty much how we all look at this point.

Hayes and Lennox sit on either side, looking like death as they text or scroll on their phones.

Gage is on the phone on the other end. He's the only one of us that doesn't look like he's knocking on death's door.

I know how this goes, so I walk to the pot of coffee and pour more into the cup next to Caius before I take his cup. The only sleep I've gotten is a few minutes in the car with my head bobbing against the headrest while we drive to the next location for Beckett to search.

But I'm thankful to always be on the move; it means he won't find me. Not that I think he'll come with the company I'm currently keeping, but I can never be too careful.

The room is full of apprehensive energy as I walk to the window to look out as I sip my coffee. Everyone is on edge from lack of sleep and concern that even if we find who took Odette, we're going to find her dead. As long as we don't find her, we can still have hope that she somehow survived her fate.

"Anything?" Beckett barks at the room.

"Corsi is looking for his daughter, but he's made no indication that he has your wife. If he had Odette, wouldn't he be trying to make a trade for his daughter back?" Lennox says.

It doesn't make sense that my father took Odette and

then didn't make contact to offer a trade or threat of some sort.

"So you think the Phantom Brotherhood has her?" Beckett asks the room.

All eyes fall, finding interest in anything—the table, coffee mugs, or phones—anything but looking at Beckett's face. The truth is they haven't found any evidence that the Phantom Brotherhood took Odette either. They've been going about their business as usual.

They gave Beckett a week to marry and arrange an alliance with my father. We are almost halfway to that point. I'm not sure anyone is worried about how they will retaliate, but Ares did say he'd take whatever Beckett loved. It would make sense that they have Odette, but it's hard to attack when we don't know Odette's location.

I know Beckett's friends haven't been able to find any clues about who took Odette either. It's like she vanished off the face of the earth. Beckett's been keeping his grief locked away, but it won't be long until it bursts out of him. I've seen grief like that. If he continues to bottle it up, when it does finally break free, it will destroy everything in its path.

I turn, and my heart pounds in my chest as all the men gaze at me. Lennox with an angry scowl like he doesn't think I belong here. Gage with curious intrigue. Hayes with a wicked longing, like he already knows he'll get into my pants someday. Caius with an almost apologetic sadness. But it's Beckett's eyes that have me captured. His eyes are blazing with grief masquerading as danger. It's fear at what he lost and might never get back.

He's the leader of the group, whether he wants to be or not. It's the reason no one has talked to me except him. He may be new to the role, and he may not have completed initiation yet, but they already follow him.

I sense what they are about to do before they do it. I know my options: freeze, fawn, fight, or flee. I get one step before the first arm grabs me, one punch in before my other arm is restrained. My only option left is to freeze—a lot of good that will do me.

10

RI

"Wakey, wakey, Princess," Lennox's voice rings in my ear.

I groan as I lift my head off a muscular shoulder and inhale a sharp whiff of aftershave. I blink slowly, my eyes struggling to open. They must have drugged me with how groggy I feel. My head starts drooping back toward the shoulder, but a hand lifts my neck up, turning me to face the other direction.

"That stuff hit you hard. You're a lightweight, Princess," Hayes says from his seat beside me. His fingers linger from my neck down the side of my breast.

"Or maybe you shouldn't drug someone who hasn't slept and has barely eaten in three days, creep."

I move to swat his hand away when I realize my hands are tied together behind my back.

"Really? Was it really necessary to tie my hands together *and* drug me?"

"Can never be too cautious, Princess," Hayes grins, wiggling his eyebrows behind his thick frames that make his eyes somehow even more dreamy. I bet the women flock to him, and I bet he breaks every one of their hearts.

"Stop calling me that." I look to Beckett, who is in the front seat of the SUV next to Caius, who's driving. I have no doubt that Beckett told them to call me Princess, knowing how much it annoys me.

"Where are we going?"

No one answers me.

"What, you didn't want to get Caius's apartment a little bloody when you torture me?"

"You're not just a pretty face. You have brains, too," Lennox snickers.

"Shut her up until we get there," Beckett orders, not even glancing back at me.

"My pleasure." Hayes plants his lips on mine. It's a violation, but I prefer it to being gagged. And as much as I hate the creep, he's a fucking good kisser. He doesn't have to force me to part my lips for his tongue, I do it automatically as his hot lips promise a good time.

There's a throat clearing, and finally, Hayes stops his kiss after swirling his tongue around my mouth one last time. He leans back in his seat with a shit-eating grin on his face.

"Poor Princess, was that your first kiss? I know your daddy doesn't let you out of your gilded cage very often."

I roll my eyes. "Considering I've already kissed two other men in this very car, no, that wasn't my first kiss."

Hayes grins wider and glances at the two in the front seat, correctly guessing which two guys I've already kissed. Caius glares at him in the rearview mirror.

I realize exactly how to play these guys. They are all hot-blooded males who think they are the shit. They all think they are the one who can get the girl. I need to play them against each other, ruin their friendships, make them all so desperate for me that they become loyal to me instead of Beckett.

I can see I already made Caius jealous by giving in to Hayes's kiss instead of resisting it. This is going to be fun. I admit it won't be hard work flirting and kissing these incredibly good-looking men.

My eyes drift to Beckett—I just wish I was able to make him jealous, make him mine. There's something about him that's different than the others. The others are younger, still focused on having fun, not settling down. Beckett is ready to devote his life to one person. He already knows how to love, and I've never seen a man love as hard as him.

The car stops, and everyone starts getting out. Lennox grabs me before Hayes has a chance to pull me out of his side of the car.

I smirk when I see his tense jaw and slits for eyes. He wasn't any more impressed with Hayes than Caius was.

Gage jumps over the middle row where we were sitting and climbs out of the car.

I raise an eyebrow when he grabs hold of my other arm. "So you're the strong, silent type. I didn't even realize you were back there."

He holds up his laptop. "Always working."

We march forward, and I look where they brought me.

"You guys must think I'm a screamer if you brought me to the middle of nowhere."

"Oh, I bet you are a screamer, Princess," Hayes trots up beside us. Caius and Beckett both walk with serious focus in front of us, not acknowledging our conversation.

Suddenly, we stop in the middle of the field. Lennox

and Gage are holding onto either of my arms, Hayes is standing to the side, and Caius and Beckett are facing us.

"You know something you aren't telling us. I'm guessing you know who has Odette and how to get her back, but if not, you have a lot more information you aren't saying," Beckett starts.

"Just torture me already if you think I have information."

"You and I both know why I can't put a mark on you."

"Daddy," Hayes taunts.

Beckett nods. "He'll punish Odette for anything I do to you whether he has her or not."

"So how do you plan on getting me to talk then, Hero?"

His eyes turn wicked, his grin devilish.

Then I feel the heat of all the guys on me.

I laugh uncontrollably.

The guys stare blankly, not understanding what's so funny.

I laugh until tears streak down my cheeks from how ridiculous they are.

"You think threatening to rape me is going to get me to talk?" I laugh manically and then stare them each down. "You have a couple of problems with your plan. One—to rape me, I would have to deny my consent, but I'd gladly fuck any of you or all of you at once. So you can't rape me."

Beckett frowns.

Caius smiles softly.

And the others' jaws drop.

"Second—you'd be doing me a favor by fucking me. I'm promised to be wed to another man. My virginity goes along with it. If one of you took it, it'd save me a lot of trouble and make my marriage alliance less valuable. In essence, it would free me."

They don't have to know if everything I'm saying is the truth, but it helps me manipulate them.

Beckett steps forward into my space. The guys' grips on my biceps tighten. My heart flutters wildly; he looks smug. *Did I make a mistake?*

"We didn't bring you here to rape you, but good to know how you feel about that." He tilts his head. "We brought you here to offer you a choice. Tell us what you know, everything you know, and you go free. There's an abandoned barn a quarter-mile from here with supplies, a car, a fake passport, everything you could possibly need to keep running."

"Or?"

"You don't tell us, and we leave you here while leaving an anonymous tip to your father. You won't make it a mile before he catches you. And once he does, he won't find any evidence that we had anything to do with your disappearance. I'm guessing spending a week back with Daddy will have you begging us to save you."

I shake my head. "I don't need you or anyone to save me."

"You sure about that, Princess? Your father taught you nothing. He kept you weak, didn't teach you how to defend yourself. You won't survive in this world without a protector."

The men are silent, waiting for me to answer.

"Tell us what you know, Ri, and you'll be free," Caius says. He's trying to be the good cop to Beckett's bad, but it won't work either.

I close my eyes, considering my options. I need to be free. I need to run. I can't go back to my father.

My head spins as I try to remember the details of the night Odette was taken. Of why I was running and what happened in the hotel, but my mind is foggy.

"Talk," Beckett orders.

I open my eyes, glaring at him. "Maybe if you hadn't drugged me, I'd have a clear head to remember."

His eyes soften just a little. He doesn't care about anything but getting Odette back.

I want to tell him. I want to tell him everything, but something in my head is preventing me from even remembering all the details.

I frown, confused. "What did you guys give me?" I yawn, growing tired again. "I need—"

Beckett grabs my face, looking at me with worry.

My legs wobble. The only things keeping me upright are Gage and Lennox.

Beckett runs his hand over my face and neck. His hand stops suddenly, and he yanks on something at the back of my neck. He releases me, and I see what's in his hand now. The dart someone shot into me knocks me out just as gunfire breaks out around us.

BECKETT

Rɪ's ᴇʏᴇs roll back in her head, and she sways on her feet just as the first fire of a gun rings out around us.

I catch her, and we all hit the ground. Gage and Lennox reach for their guns and start firing back. I can't see what Caius or Hayes are doing behind me, but I do know that these guys are friends who have worked together for years. Even though they want me to be their leader, they can communicate in this moment a lot better without me barking orders at them.

My task is getting the girl to safety. She was going to talk, and then they hit her with that damn dart. I was so close to getting information that could help me find Odette.

Gage meets my gaze.

"You guys get rid of the threat. I'm going to get Princess to safety," I say.

He nods. "Take the car. We'll find you when we're finished." He whistles at Caius, who tosses me the keys. Gage meets Lennox's eyes. "Go on my count."

I kneel over Ri, ready to toss her over my back when

the men cover us. I just hope they're as good as I've been told, because I'll have no way to defend us. With only one arm, I'll have no way to hold a gun while carrying Ri.

Gage and Lennox pop up at the same time. "Go!"

I toss Ri over my shoulder in one swoop and start running toward the car as fast as I can. The ground is uneven under my feet, but I don't stop running. Every shot sparks fear into my heart—*did they hit Ri and destroy my best chance at finding Odette?* But the guys must be doing a good job at diverting their fire because I can feel Ri's heavy breathing against my back as I run.

I don't know who's attacking us, but I assume it's Ri's father. The Phantom Brotherhood wouldn't attack until my week is up. Nevertheless, I need to get all the information I can get from Princess before I give her back.

I reach the driver's door and throw it open before diving us both into the front seat. Ri rolls off my shoulder, and I shove her hard into the passenger seat. Her head hits the passenger window with a thud.

I start the car, and I pull out my gun, holding it against the wheel. I look in the rearview mirror and see men attacking from behind us as well.

"Shit."

I consider my options and decide our best escape route is forward. It also gives me a chance to pick up the rest of the guys.

I slam on the gas, and we jerk forward. Ri moans in her seat next to me.

Shots ring out, and I swerve the car before pushing Ri's head down in her seat to keep her safe. She groans louder.

I reach Hayes first, who turns as he hears me approach. When he sees that it's me, I stop the car for half a second, and he swings open the passenger door and climbs in. He uses his body to shield Ri as he hangs out the window to continue firing.

I glare at him out of the corner of my eye.

When the shooting dies down, and we continue driving, he notices. "Don't worry, I won't kiss her again. Don't get your panties all in a bunch." He fires a couple of shots. "I'm not sure why you care about her, though, not when you have Odette. But Ri was into a six-way if you want to try that out with us."

I swerve, and his head slams into the roof of the car.

"Jesus Christ, it was a joke."

I roll my eyes. I doubt Princess would be up for a six-way if it came down to it, especially if she is a virgin like she claims. She just has a big mouth that gets her into trouble.

We pick up Gage next, who hops into the back seat behind me. "They're falling back."

"Do you think it's Corsi?" I ask as I continue to drive, noticing less gunfire than before.

"No, if this was Corsi, we'd all be dead."

I frown.

"How's Princess?" I ask Hayes.

He pulls himself back in through the window and checks on her. "Still breathing, still unconscious. That dart wasn't in her long, though. I doubt she got a full dose of whatever it was. She'll come to soon."

"Just make sure she stays alive." I drive faster until I see Lennox crouched down and shooting from behind a large tree stump.

"Knox!" Gage shouts as he opens the rear passenger door. Lennox runs and dives into the back of the car as I roll through his area slowly and punch the gas.

"Where's Caius?" I ask. Now that I've collected three of them, Caius doesn't stand a chance unless we get him.

"He took off running as a distraction while you ran with Ri," Lennox answers out of breath.

"Shit."

I keep driving, but the gunfire has mostly stopped at this point. I can't believe that whoever attacked us was thwarted by the four of them. By the amount of gunfire I heard, I know they had us outnumbered. I look in my rearview mirror but don't see any cars following us anymore.

The tension in the car pulses like a war drum. Everyone is holding their gun while barely breathing. We all feel the strange silence, a looming threat warning that we're driving into a trap.

"Holy fuck," Hayes says.

All of our eyes travel forward until we spot it. A dozen cars. Thirty-plus men. And Caius bloodied with a gun pointed at his head.

"We should turn back," Gage says, his eyes traveling from me to Ri.

I know that's the best way to save Ri, but if we did that, we'd be leaving Caius for dead. I may not have known these guys long, and I may not want to be their leader, but I do know that I have a responsibility to everyone in this car. But making decisions like this when there is no right answer is one of the many reasons I never wanted to lead.

"Keep Ri down so they don't see her." I roll the car to a stop a few yards away from the line of men. I pop my car door open and start walking slowly toward the men who are holding Caius hostage. The rest of the men don't need orders to know that they should follow me. I hear their doors slam shut and the heavy crunch of their footsteps as we walk forward as a group. We hold our guns at our sides, knowing that if we open fire, we are all sitting ducks.

A man near Caius asks, "You in charge?"

I nod solemnly.

"Give us the girl, and we'll give you back your guy in one piece."

"Who is us?" I ask, wanting to know their affiliation.

The guys are staring him down, snarling, and growling. I'm pretty sure at this point, I'm the only one who doesn't know who these men are.

"Ask one of your guard dogs," he snaps back, proving me right. The guys now recognize our attackers.

Caius's face is covered in blood, and his head is drooped against his chest. He tries to lift his head but doesn't have the strength. I have no doubt that if I leave him with them, he'll be dead shortly.

"What will it be? Trade or do we have to kill you all in order to get her?"

I scan them all, looking for a way out.

"Don't do it, don't trade," Caius says, still not lifting his head.

The guys tense next to me, but none of them speak. They're waiting for me to decide.

Do I let Caius die and keep Ri? Or do I give them Ri and get us all out of here safely?

"Trade me," Ri says, stomping toward us.

We all turn in her direction. "What the hell are you doing?"

"Saving your asses." She shakes her head as she walks to me. "I'll tell you everything I know if you are up for playing hero later." She winks at me.

I frown.

She starts walking forward, but I grab her arm,

yanking her ear against my lips. "Don't die, Princess. We aren't finished with you yet." Then I push her toward the men.

"Let's trade."

The second I release Ri, the man holding a gun to Caius's head pushes him toward us. We all want to get out of here without any more bloodshed.

Hayes is closest to Caius and grabs onto his friend.

"No, don't..." Caius mumbles, but his words are barely coherent.

We all start walking back to our car while a man grabs Ri and points a gun at her head. Her arms are still tied behind her back. She turns her eyes toward mine just before she's shoved into the back of an SUV. Her eyes are full of threat about what will happen if I don't come save her. She doesn't have to threaten me. She's the only one who has a clue where and how to get Odette back. She's shoved into the car, and we hop back into ours.

I throw the car in reverse and get the hell out of here.

"Who the hell are they?"

"Mayhem," Lennox answers.

"What the hell does Mayhem want with Ri?"

"The same thing the Phantom Brotherhood wants, I'm guessing. She's a mafia princess, and the key to controlling Corsi is controlling her."

"Now what? Are we going to save Princess or are we going to find another way to find Odette?" Hayes asks.

That's the question.

All the men stare at me with such longing in their eyes. They want to go save Ri. If it wasn't for Caius bleeding all over the backseat of the car, I'd guess they would want me to chase after them right now.

I have an urge to go after them—it's deep and feral.

And it's taking everything inside of me to keep driving away from Ri. I keep glancing into my rearview mirror, hoping she somehow escaped and is running after us.

But of course she didn't escape. She's just a feisty princess with a smart mouth. I'm sure her father paid for the finest dresses and lessons on which fork to use at the dinner table—nothing that could help her defend herself.

It doesn't explain why I have this intense urge to turn the car around, though. I don't care what happens to that girl. The only reason I care is because she's our best lead at finding Odette.

My phone buzzes in my pocket. I yank it out and read the message.

Langston: We found a video of Odette.

My heart stops.

I hold the phone against the steering wheel and quickly type back.

Me: Is she alive?

Langston: Yes.

"How are you feeling, Caius? Should we find a hospital?" Gage asks.

"No, I'm sure I have a concussion. Just put some gauze or stitches or whatever we have on my head, and let's go get Ri." His eyes meet mine in the rearview mirror.

I try not to react, but I'm not a very good actor.

"We have to go get Ri! We can't save my sister, but we can save her. No other innocent person deserves to die. We can stop them from hurting her!" he yells at me.

"Actually, Odette's alive."

Caius's mouth falls open. "Odette's...alive?"

I nod.

"They're taking Ri to a cabin near the lake. If you want to follow them, turn left. Where is Odette?" Gage asks, typing on his phone. He must have put a tracker on Ri when she was unconscious.

"The last video we have of her is in the city," I say.

I pause at the fork in the road. *Do I turn right or left? Do I go after Ri or Odette?*

Odette is my choice, but I'm not sure I can get her back without Ri. And yet, I can't stand to leave Odette alone for another second. If I have a chance to get her back now, I have to try.

"Left or right? Who are we going after, boss?" Gage asks.

I look in each of the men's eyes in the car, looking for guidance. For once, I don't want to be the one making the decision. Caius opens his mouth. He's their former leader, and he's emotionally invested in this.

But Hayes grabs the first aid kit and starts working on the gash on Caius's head. Hayes shakes his head at Caius, and he doesn't speak up.

They are letting me decide. And I have no doubt that if I fuck this up, I won't just lose Odette; I'll lose them all.

It was my plan to bring Ri here, to persuade her to talk. I fucked it up. If I fuck up again, I doubt they will continue to follow me whether I married Odette or not.

I don't have time to think about which is the best option. I have to decide. I turn the wheel, and I drive in the direction my gut is telling me to go.

I FEEL like a criminal being arrested as I'm pushed into the backseat of the blacked-out SUV. My eyes cling to Beckett's until the very last second. I should look into all of the men's eyes—Hayes, Gage, Lennox, and Caius, not just Beckett's. Beckett hates me and blames me for Odette being taken.

The other guys are who I should be focused on. I've kissed two of them, and Gage seems interested, but Lennox is too angry to care about me. I should have spent more time convincing them to save me, because I'm not sure if Beckett will. My only value to him is if I can convince him that I can help him get Odette back.

Two men climb into the front seat and start driving. My head is spinning as we drive, but I'm shocked that no one is in the backseat next to me, ensuring that I don't escape. They must really think I'm not a threat—which I guess is true. My arms are still tied behind my back, my head is throbbing, I can barely keep my eyes open, and my stomach feels like I'll vomit at any second. Even if I was perfectly clear-headed, my arms were untied, and I had a gun, I still wouldn't have a clue how to escape. I don't have any training or any experience using a gun. My father preferred I was weak and dependent on men. Just another reason I hate him.

"Who are you guys?"

The guy in the passenger seat flips on the radio.

"Did my father send you?"

He turns the volume up. Clearly, I'm not going to get any answers.

I focus on the roads, trying to figure out where we are going while I work on the rope tying my hands together. After struggling for twenty minutes, I think I've only managed to get the rope twisted tighter around my wrists and given myself rope burn.

I sigh and relax my head back, closing my eyes. My only option now is to try to regain my strength and hope that Beckett and the guys are close behind us. I don't want a hero; I want to save my damn self, but I'm not strong enough.

If I ever get out of here, that's going to change. I'm taking every self-defense and weapons training class I can find. I won't be weak ever again. I won't have to sit around and wait for a man to save me.

I must fall asleep because when I open my eyes, we're parked at what looks to be a cabin in the woods near a lake.

"Get out, whore," a man says as he throws open my door and grabs my bicep, not giving me any time to comprehend what's happening.

"You could ask nicely; no need to call me names."

He snickers. "Why? That's what you are—a dirty whore. Don't think we didn't notice how those men protected you. You must be sucking all of their dicks to get protection like that."

I roll my eyes as the man with a twisted front tooth, hairy arms, and a broad chest walks me up the three steps to the cabin door. If only Beckett and his men were protecting me because they cared about me and not because I'm the only clue to finding Odette. Hairy arms here must have missed the part where they drugged me, tied me up, and threatened me in the middle of nowhere. Beckett and his guys might want to fuck me, but they don't care about me. *And why should they?* They don't even know me.

So why did you offer yourself up to save Caius's life?

Because then he'll owe me.

The man pounds on the door, and only then do I realize he's not in charge. I don't think any of the men who kidnapped me are.

The door opens. "You succeeded."

"Your princess, as requested." He shoves me inside, and I stumble, almost falling flat on my face. A pair of strong hands catches me from falling face-first onto the wooden floor.

Slowly, I look up and meet his cruel eyes, instantly realizing I've made a terrible mistake. I should have let Caius die. Whatever this stranger has planned for me, I won't survive it.

He glowers, licking his bottom lip like I'm a meal he plans on devouring.

"Good job, Eric, I can take it from here." His eyes twinkle with disgusting thoughts as his eyes plainly roam my body. This man is easily two decades older than me. He has crow's feet around his eyes, several gray hairs in his medium brown hair, and faded tattoos all over his body.

He's fit, but not as fit as the guys. I'm guessing he's the kind of leader who sits back and lets his men do all of the dirty work.

"I'm going to have so much fun with you." He grabs my hair, fisting it in a ponytail and yanking on my head.

I grit my teeth to keep from giving him the satisfaction of hearing me groan in pain. He drags me through the small cabin that seems to be empty except for the two of us.

"Your organization must suck if this is all you can afford."

He stops suddenly, and my head rams into his ass before I can stop my forward momentum. He yanks my head up until he's breathing hot vile breath against my lips.

"You think those boys are going to save you? I have two decades of experience on them. There is a reason we are in a cabin in the middle of fucking nowhere and not in my mansion near the city. They'll come for you. You're a pretty plaything, and men don't like to share their playthings with others." One of his hands runs down my cheek, and I try to bite it off.

He grins. "But know this—they'll be too late when they finally come."

"So you plan on killing me?"

He tilts his head as his smile reaches his eyes. "Now, why would I do that when you are so much more useful to me alive?"

"I don't understand. If you aren't going to kill me, it will never be too late to save me."

He shakes his head. "Your father taught you so little. When I marry you, it will be too late. You'll be mine. I'll own you. I'll have the power of not only my men but your father's men behind me too. Your boys won't stand a chance."

I laugh. "All of you are fucking insane if you think my father will form an alliance with you just because you married me. My father hates me. He's been trying to sell me off since my eighteenth birthday. All he wants is money and power. He won't give you any of it just because you make yourself my husband."

He grabs my chin with a wicked snicker. "Your father really didn't tell you, did he?"

I swallow hard as I feel my pulse in my throat. *What didn't my father tell me?* He told me nothing except that he would choose my husband. This man isn't the man my father chose. These men can fight over me all they want, but I will never consent to marry any of them. And more importantly to me, my father won't consent either. Even if I legally marry another man, my father will make sure the marriage is never valid. That's how much power he has. So as much as I'd love to choose the man I marry, I can't.

"I'll never marry you."

He smashes his lips over mine.

I fight. My arms struggle to get free from the rope behind me, but it just digs tighter into my wrists. I try to pull my head back, but his hand is wrapped around the back of my head. I want to open my lips to bite down on his and make him bleed, but I'm afraid if I open my mouth, his tongue will slither its way in. So I keep my lips squeezed closed; that is until he punches me in the gut.

I exhale a sharp breath as my lungs burn for air. He takes the opportunity to shove his tongue deep into my throat before I catch my breath. I try to bite down, but his hand on my jaw keeps it open.

"You'll marry me, Princess."

"I won't. There is nothing you can threaten me with. There is no one that I love. And I know you won't kill me. You can't if you want my father to align with you."

"Everyone has someone they love, even if they don't realize it. I'll find your weakness. You love yourself, if not someone else. I may not kill you, but I can make your life a living hell. You may think you can handle torture, but I doubt you can withstand much pain. You'll cave before the night is out."

"Who are you?"

"Paxton Cook, leader of Mayhem."

If I had been taught anything about the world I live in, then maybe his name would mean something to me. But since my father left me a fool, I don't know how seriously to take his threats.

"Come now, Rialta; it's time to get ready. We have a wedding we don't want to be late for."

He once again grabs my hair and pulls me forward. I move my feet quickly to keep him from tearing my hair out. He drags me into the bedroom, kicks the door shut, and then releases me.

I stand up cautiously as I look around the room. There is a queen-sized bed with a multi-colored quilt as the comforter, a deer head hanging over the bed, and a bible lying on the table in the corner. I suspect that this property doesn't belong to Paxton.

I scan to see an open bathroom door, and then my breath whooshes out of me as I see a big, puffy white dress hanging in front of the closet door.

Holy hell, he really does think I'll marry him.

"You might as well just forge the papers now, because I'll never marry you. No need to pretend by forcing me into a dress. It's not happening."

"Now, who would believe I married the mafia princess while she was wearing some other guy's sweatshirt? We have to do this properly for it to be believed."

"No one will believe I married you."

"They will. Because by the time I'm through with you, you'll be begging to become my wife." He casually struts past me and enters the bathroom, leaving me alone in the bedroom.

I run to the door and then turn around so my still bound hands can open the door. The door falls open, and I tumble out with it.

"Where are you going, Princess?" the hairy armed man from before says, looking down at me with a rotten smile.

He grabs my bicep and yanks me up. "You're not allowed to leave this room until you are dressed. If you come out again before you're dressed, I'll shoot you." He shoves me back into the room. I fall on my ass as he slams the door in my face.

Shit.

I push myself back to my feet to try the window. But when I reach it, I see the dozens of men pacing outside.

Fuck!

I'm trapped. There is no way I can escape that many men. I'm not even sure Beckett's guys are going to be able to defeat so many.

"Rialta, it's time for your bath," Paxton's voice carries through the open door of the bathroom. It's then that I hear the running water.

A shiver runs down my spine, and my legs tremble. I understand now what he meant about the boys not being able to save me.

Paxton emerges from the bathroom.

I keep the fear away from my face and out of my voice. "Untie me so I can bathe."

He chuckles. "I'll untie you when you consent to being my wife. Although, I may have to fuck you tied up first."

I cringe. I can't hide my disgust, which only pleases him. This man is a sadist. He gets off on torturing others. He's not like others that just want the power.

He prowls toward me. I take a step back between the bed and the window. I keep walking back, stalling, trying to look for a weapon I can use. But even if I find a knife or a gun in the nightstand that I eventually bump into, it's not much use to me with my arms tied behind my back.

Fucking Beckett. If it wasn't for him, my arms wouldn't be tied behind my back, and maybe I'd be able to defend myself.

Paxton stops as I'm backed into the corner of the room. "I'm curious; what are you planning on doing now? You have no weapon, no escape. Corsi may be smart, but he raised a fool for a daughter."

I can't argue with that. I'm a fool for ever thinking I could run from my fate.

He grabs my arm and drags me into the bathroom. At least he didn't grab my hair this time.

The bathroom is small. It has an oval-shaped metal tub, a toilet, and a sink. There's no window in here, no escape.

Paxton reaches for the hem of my sweatshirt, and I wonder how he's going to take it off with my hands tied behind me. He pulls it over my head, then spins me around. I suck in a sharp breath as a knife slices into the sweatshirt and then grazes my skin.

"Oops, did I hit too deep?"

"Asshole," I mumble under my breath.

He chuckles. "You're a fool with a smart mouth that's going to get you killed someday. I may be your husband by the end of the night, but I won't be rescuing you when you inevitably get yourself in trouble. You'll do well to remember that and keep your mouth shut if you want to survive."

"What if I don't want to survive? What if I want to die and bring you down with me?"

He rips the sweatshirt from my body until I'm standing in a bra and boxer shorts, my arms still tied behind my back. His hand brushes my side across the piece of gauze over my wound. He handles me roughly, wanting me to prove him right—that I do want to live. That I can't handle pain and torture. I don't allow my body to react to his painful touch.

His hands grip my boobs through my bra, and I flinch, trying to jerk out of his grasp. He lets me with a loud snicker. "You want to live. You want to survive. You're just like every other creature on earth that wants to avoid pain. When the time comes, you'll be saying 'I do' to me to avoid torture. If you want me to fuck you quickly to consummate our marriage, I suggest you go along with my plans."

Paxton has found my weakness. I don't mind physical pain, but to be raped and violated is different. It's something I'll avoid at all costs.

"Now, turn back around."

Slowly, I do as I'm told without mouthing off again. Pulsing anxiety spreads through my body like wildfire as I realize what trading my life for Caius's really meant. The guys may eventually save me, not because they care about me but because of Odette.

But when they do, it could be too late—not too late to reverse the marriage, rather too late to save my soul. I'll be lost if he rapes me. Some women come back from being violated, but I'd rather die.

His hands grip my boxers and panties beneath them. He slides them down over my hips until they fall free to the floor.

I hold my breath, trying to keep the panic at bay as I feel his hands at my back, undoing my bra and then slicing through the shoulder straps with his knife. My eyes bulge in horror as I watch my bra fall to the floor.

I'm not ashamed of my body. I like how I look, and being practically naked in front of Caius or Beckett wasn't a problem. I enjoyed the attention, but I don't want to feel Paxton's eyes on me.

"Get in the bath."

My shoulders shudder. He's looking at my back, but once I climb in the tub, he'll be able to see everything.

His hands are on my hips, and he starts sliding them up toward my breasts again. I jump out of my skin, trying to clamber into the tub, causing me to make a huge splash as my body lands awkwardly in the water.

His vicious laugh rings in my ears, and I feel my tears welling.

You're stronger than this. You always knew your body would be sold to a man one day. This won't break you.

I replay those words in my head, while refusing to look at Paxton. But I don't need to see him to feel the heat of his eyes on me like a peeping tom. I can't move with my arms tied behind my back. The water causes the rope to rub more roughly against my wrists, so every movement burns. I glance down at my side and am surprised that my side doesn't hurt from getting wet. Soaking in the tub can't be good for my stitches, but surprisingly it doesn't sting. *Maybe the drugs are still numbing me?*

Paxton grabs the bottle of shampoo next to the tub, squirts some on my hair, and then starts massaging my scalp.

I clench my teeth together and squeeze my eyes shut. He's just touching my hair, and already my body feels like it's on fire.

Just pretend you're at the beauty salon. It's nice that someone else is washing your hair. Jan is washing your hair, not this sick prick.

"You have such beautiful hair and an even more beautiful body. No wonder your father keeps you locked away. Men would fight to the death to have you."

"You're going to die whether you have me or not."

Water crashes over my face as he dunks me under the water. I wasn't expecting it, so some of the water goes up my nose. A few seconds later, he lets me up.

I cough up water as my head resurfaces.

He grabs my chin and turns it toward me. "I'm going to enjoy breaking you, Princess. But know this—you're mine now, and I don't plan on dying for a long, long time."

He dunks me under water again. This time, I'm ready. I surrender to the feeling of the water as an escape from him. When he pulls me back up, it's too soon. I'd rather stay under the water.

He grabs the bar of soap next, and my body seizes. He starts at my shoulders and works down to my chest. His eyes darken, and drool pools at the corners of his mouth as he rubs the bar over my breasts and nipples. His hand slides hungrily down my stomach and between my legs.

A tear rolls down my cheek, but otherwise, I don't let the fear in. Paxton is a dead man. I'll kill him for this. And if he violates me more, I'll get him back for everything he does first, and then I'll kill him.

The sick fucker takes his time mainly washing my breasts and between my legs. Apparently, my arms and legs don't need washing. When he's finished, he grabs my bicep and pulls me up before wrapping a towel around my body.

"Did you hire anyone to do my hair and makeup?" I ask, hoping now that he's touched my body, he'll leave me alone to get dressed and have my hair and makeup done. It will give me time to figure out how to kill him. I won't leave here alive unless the guys find a way to save me, but I can ensure Paxton dies.

"And why would I do that?"

"You know how to do hair and makeup?"

"I'm the groom, and I know what I like. Since my opinion is all that matters, I'll be the one doing your hair and makeup."

"Oh, it's because you're poor and don't have any money. That's why you're doing this."

Slap.

My head whips to the side. My nostrils flare as I breathe deeply and angrily, turning my head back to face him.

"Watch your mouth...or don't." He shrugs.

He pulls me out of the tub and then begins drying me with the towel, once again paying special attention to my boobs and pussy. I bite my tongue the entire time to keep from saying something that will get me slapped again.

He walks me back to the bedroom and tells me to sit on the edge of the bed. I do, trying my best not to shiver, still completely naked. He enters the bathroom and comes back with a blow dryer.

He blow-dries my hair straight and then surprisingly is able to apply a good amount of makeup to my face. It wouldn't be so bad if I wasn't naked, my cheeks weren't flush, my skin wasn't crawling, and my blood pressure wasn't spiking to dangerous levels. He finishes my hair and tops my head with a tiara.

"Time to get dressed."

He walks over to the closet, where a very large fluffy white dress hangs. It's the opposite of a dress I would choose for my wedding. It's a complete princess dress, and despite what everyone calls me, I'm not a princess. If I were to ever want to get married, I'd probably wear black or red, anything but traditional virgin white.

He pulls the dress off the hanger and walks over to me. It's a strapless dress, so he won't have to remove the rope tying my hands together.

I sigh.

He holds the dress out for me to step into. I guess I don't get to wear underwear or a bra. I step into the tent of a dress, and then he pulls it up. He circles behind me so he can zip it up.

"Beautiful."

My eyes water.

"Now, don't go crying on me and ruin my masterpiece."

I growl.

He snickers; his eyes are roaming over every inch of my body like I already belong to him.

"I'm going to go change, and then we can get married. There are guards outside your door. Don't try anything, and don't ruin my work." He walks to the door and pauses.

"Or maybe do." He winks sadistically at me.

I continue biting my tongue so hard that it bleeds as I watch him finally leave me alone.

The second he closes the door, I run to the drawers

looking for anything I can use as a weapon to kill him. The drawers have a couple of condoms, a notepad, and a pen—nothing I could use to kill him. I throw the closet door open, but all I find are clothes. I run to the bathroom and pull open every drawer—toothpaste, a comb, floss, nothing useful.

"Fuck." I slam the drawer shut, my eyes catching in the mirror.

That's when I take the time to finally look at myself. I'm shocked by what I see. My shiny dark hair with a tiara, cat eye makeup, red lips, and my cleavage spilling over the top of the dress. I look like a teenager about to go to prom, not a sexy woman in control of her own body.

But that's what he wants to make me feel like. He owns me, and I'm a scared little girl instead of the warrior badass I want to be.

I hear the door open, and I tear my gaze from the mirror as Paxton enters. "Admiring my work? I did a good job, didn't I?"

I don't answer.

He walks over to me and hooks his arm through mine. "Come on, it's time to get married."

RI

I DON'T KNOW where I was expecting to get married, but it wasn't this. Paxton leads me out of the cabin, down a trail to the water, and onto a small dock where a man with a bible waits at the end. His men surround the edges of the water, but only two walk onto the dock with us.

One of the men holds up a phone, and it's then that I realize he's recording this. I don't know what they expect is going to happen when they show this video to my father. I don't think he'll be too happy to see I'm tied up, but then again, he doesn't actually care about me. He would just see it as a big f-u to him that Paxton would dare to tie up and marry his daughter without his permission.

The officiant starts talking, while Paxton continues to hold onto my arm like this is a real wedding and not forced at all.

"Repeat after me," the officiant says, and then I have to listen to Paxton declare his devotion to me like he's been waiting his entire life for me. I guess in some ways he has been looking for a meal ticket like me his whole life.

Paxton stops talking and looks at me expectantly. I wasn't listening, so I don't know what words to say.

"Say, 'I, Rialta Corsi, take Paxton Cook as my husband,'" Paxton says through gritted teeth, already losing patience with me.

"No."

"You don't get to say no. This isn't your choice. Say the words!"

My eyes flutter to the officiant, who doesn't seem fazed at all. I give him a smug smile. He's dressed in a simple suit. I'm not sure if he is a man of the church or just someone who works for Paxton who got ordained online. Either way, he doesn't seem surprised by my noncompliance.

Paxton grabs my throat and squeezes, immediately cutting off my supply of oxygen. My eyes bulge, but I force myself to remain calm, not to react. He won't kill me. He needs me alive in order to marry me and take whatever power he thinks my father will provide.

So despite the strong urge in my body to fight for air, I remain still. It's painful, not just in my throat, but in my lungs, too, as the remainder of my oxygen slips from my body.

Finally, Paxton releases my throat, and I gulp down large mouthfuls of air as I bend over. Paxton's satisfied smirk beams down at me.

"Let's try this again. I, Rialta, take Paxton as my husband. I shortened it to make it easier for you to remember."

I stand up tall. "I, Rialta, am going to kill you. That's a promise."

Paxton's eyes darken with fury, and then they snap to one of his men standing on the pier.

I feel the crack of a whip before I see it. It slices through my skin, and I can't help the cry that escapes my lips. I almost stumble over from the impact. My arms still being tied behind my back doesn't make staying on my feet any easier; neither do the heels I'm balancing precariously in.

Paxton nods, and the whip bursts against my skin once again. I'm ready for the impact this time, but the burning sting is worse now that my skin is so sensitive. I have no idea if the whip broke my skin. *Are there just welts, or am I bleeding?*

"I'm sure my father is going to find this wedding valid after he sees you whipping me into submission." My eyes throw daggers at the man still recording us.

"Your father will see what we want him to see."

He's going to alter the video to make it look like I'm a willing participant. If my father sees that, he'll kill me himself for disobeying him and marrying without his permission.

The whip comes down on me again, this time missing my back and striking my hands. I crumble to my knees as the pain hits my palms and shoots through my body. I scream, not out of pain but out of frustration for my life.

How did I end up here? Even if I escape with my life, my body not violated, and single, it doesn't change anything. I'm still running. I'll still end up married to a man I hate— a man who only sees me as property.

"Are you ready to cooperate now?" Paxton asks, assuming my posture means I'm broken and defeated, not furious and more willing to fight than I have been before.

I push myself back onto my feet as I let my strength rise in my chest. I smile like he's made me happier than I ever thought possible, and then I snap. I run full speed at

Paxton, and my head rams into his stomach. I knock him off the edge of the dock and into the water.

The men chuckle at first until Paxton's head pops up out of the water. His nostrils flare as he snorts water out of his nose. The men fall silent instantly, seeing the rage on their boss' face.

One of his men runs down the dock to offer his hand to help him out of the water, but Paxton brushes it away before pulling himself up the side of the dock.

I bob my head suddenly toward him to headbutt him again, but the man who had offered to help Paxton up pulls me back. Paxton removes his jacket and then shakes like a wet dog.

"Should I get you a towel?" the man gripping my arm asks.

"No," Paxton growls. He walks over to the man holding the whip and takes it from him. "Hold her."

Both men move to my sides, gripping my biceps and forcing me into a kneeling position.

Paxton hits me wildly over and over, his strokes hitting all over my back and neck. Tears sting my eyes, as I realize these whips are causing my skin to break open. I clench my teeth together to prevent a whimper of pain from escaping.

I hear Paxton panting behind me as he exerts all his energy striking me.

"Sir?"

The voice gets Paxton to stop. I'm still hunched over as tears and mascara stream down my face. Paxton may have done a good job with my makeup, but he didn't ensure my mascara was waterproof. I sniffle back snot and tears as I'm pulled to my feet, hoping to hide some of the pain that has marred my face.

"You can whip me to within an inch of my life and I still won't say the words to marry you."

"That's why we've decided to take a different route," Paxton says confidently.

That's when I see who his men are leading down the dock—Caius Monroe. His hands are tied behind his back like mine, and two men stand on either side of him. Other than a shiner around his eye and a gash that has already been stitched up on his head, he looks unharmed.

The men stop near us at the end of the dock. Paxton immediately pulls out his gun and aims it at Caius, not even looking him in the face.

"Now, this is how it's going to work. You are going to repeat the words the officiant says, or I'll kill him. Understand?"

I don't look at Caius, and I don't react. "What makes you think I care about this man?"

"You traded your life to save his."

"If you didn't notice, I was a captive with them. They were the ones who tied my arms together and drugged me. I already knew how dangerous they were; I was hoping I had a better chance at escaping you than them. That's why I traded my life."

"I don't believe you."

I hold my breath, trying to figure out what to do. I don't want to marry Paxton, *but does it really matter if I say the words?* If my father isn't happy with the marriage, he'll get it annulled. And by saying the words, I could save Caius's life.

But I really hate losing. I hate being manipulated. And once I'm married, Paxton will complete his threat and rape me. There will be no one to save me then.

Paxton hits Caius over the head with the butt of his gun.

I wince.

It's enough for Paxton to beam with confidence in his plan. I do care about Caius. He hands his gun off to one of his men before pulling a handkerchief out of his pocket and dabbing at my face.

"You ruined my masterpiece. Just one of the many things you'll be punished for later." When he's finished wiping the ruined makeup from my face, he runs his hand through his own hair, slicking it back. Then he turns me so my back is away from the camera. He holds me around the waist, so close that with the right camera angle, I'm sure you can't tell that my arms are tied behind my back or that my back is coated in blood.

"You may start again, Richard," Paxton says.

The officiant starts speaking again like the last twenty minutes haven't even occurred. "Please repeat after me: 'I, Rialta Corsi, take Paxton Cook as my husband.'"

I lick my lips, considering my options before I say the words. But I don't know how to save myself from this fate. I can save Caius, though.

"I do this and you let him go free. You don't go after him or his friends, agreed?"

A deal made with the devil is not likely to be kept, but I have to try. If I know that my loss will at least help them, I can live with it. If Odette is alive, she deserves to have her brother, her husband, and his friends alive when she returns.

"Of course," Paxton says.

Yea, I don't believe him. But I'm sure there will be plenty more deals he makes with me when he needs me to agree to something. Caius is too useful as a bargaining chip, so

Paxton won't kill him, but he also won't let him go. For now, keeping him alive is the best I can do.

I suck in a deep breath and nod, glancing at Caius out of the corner of my eye.

Caius winks, or at least I think he winks at me. *Is he thanking me for saving his life? Something else? Did I imagine it?*

I push the illusion out of my head. "I—I, Rialta Corsi, take Paxton Cook to be..." Paxton's eyebrows raise in anticipation. "To be my husband."

The officiant starts talking again, but Paxton leans into my ear. "Good girl."

I swallow my disgust and glance at our surroundings —the incredible view of the lake, the forest, trees, flowers, the sun setting. I can't imagine a more perfect place for a wedding. If I were to get married for real, I would want it to be in nature like this. But instead, this place will haunt my dreams.

"I now declare you husband and wife."

I'm pretty sure he skipped a few steps, but they must be satisfied with what I said. Paxton yanks me flush to his body and then presses a rough kiss to my lips, smearing his saliva all over my mouth.

I hear a single gunshot.

I try to push Paxton away, hoping like hell his men didn't already betray me by shooting Caius. But when I do, Caius is running toward us.

Caius grabs me just as I turn to look at Paxton and see blood spilling from his mouth. He was the one shot.

"What's—?" I start to question as Caius grabs me with unbound hands, throws me over his shoulder, runs the few feet off the end of the dock, and then jumps.

We both splash hard into the water, and our bodies

disconnect. My hands are still tied, so I start kicking, but I'm not sure if surfacing right away is the best idea.

I open my eyes in the murky water and see Caius grab my arm as he begins to swim, pulling me along behind him. As I guessed, he doesn't surface right away.

We swim as far as our lungs will allow us, and then we break for the surface. Neither of us stop as our heads finally push high enough above the water to take a breath. Even though our lungs are begging for us to stop and take a long, deep breath, we continue swimming because our lives depend on it. Caius grips my arm and pulls me along behind him, while I kick as hard as I can.

"Almost there," he says.

I don't have a clue what he means. We are swimming toward the middle of the lake. There is no land in sight. We can't stop swimming anytime soon unless we want to drown. But then I hear the buzz of an engine, and I see a speedboat to our left, driving toward us at full speed. The boat comes to a stop in front of us, and then Hayes reaches down to lift me up out of the water with one tug of his arm. I collapse onto Hayes's body on the deck. Gage helps Caius out of the water, and then the boat starts speeding off, making it impossible to stand up.

"I love you on top of me, Princess, but you're bleeding, and I can't breathe," Hayes says.

Gage helps me stand. "I'll go get the first aid kit."

"Here, let me get those ropes off you. They have to be killing your wrists," Hayes says.

"Ropes you assholes put on," I remind them.

Hayes winces.

Caius looks like he's going to be sick as he watches Hayes slice through the ropes and gently pulls them off. A layer of my skin goes with the rope, but I'm still thankful to be free.

Gage walks around my back and freezes. His eyes bulge as he looks at my back.

"If you think that's bad, you should see the other guy," I joke.

But the guys don't laugh. Gage hands the first aid kit to Caius, and then he stomps off.

"What's wrong with him?" I ask.

Caius shakes his head. "Sit here." He pats the bench in the front of the boat. I straddle the bench while Hayes sits facing me and Caius sits behind me.

Caius holds out some pain pills to me, which I swallow dry. Then he holds out the first aid kit to Hayes, who digs through it, finding what he needs before Caius sets the box on the bench between us.

"This might sting," Hayes says.

I nod and hold out my wrists, and he dabs the wounds on my wrists with alcohol to clean them.

I hiss, not caring if I come across as a wimp. Last time I was in this position, I was brave and stone-faced, but now I'm pissed. I was about to be married off and raped because these jackasses decided to tie me up and take me to the middle of nowhere to get answers instead of just talking to me.

Hayes's face drops with concern. "I'm sorry."

"You should be," I snap back.

Hayes frowns. "I know."

He continues in silence, wrapping gauze around my wrists until my wounds are covered. He studies his work for a second, then he stands. He looks at me like he wants to say something more. The pain is clear on his face from his furrowed brows and clenched jaw. Whatever is on his mind, he doesn't say. Instead, he walks toward the back of the boat, where I assume the rest of the guys are, leaving Caius and me alone.

I shiver despite the sun warming the water off my skin.

"Do you want a towel?"

"No." A towel would only cling to my back where my wounds are. It wouldn't help.

I turn to look at Caius. He's removed his shirt, his abs glistening under the sunlight and still soaking wet.

"I—uh—I need to clean your wounds. Then I can apply a cold compress that will help with the pain," Caius stutters. I don't know why these guys have all suddenly lost their balls, but they are all walking on eggshells around me. None of them able to say what they really want to.

I face forward out at the lake as Caius begins. I wince every time he touches me. I whine, I complain, I wiggle, I make his job as difficult as possible.

Caius eventually finishes and occupies Hayes's spot in front of me. He carefully takes my hands in his.

"I'm so sorry. I—"

I open my mouth, but Caius puts his fingers over my lips, silencing me.

"I need to get this out. I'm so sorry. This is all my fault. Your back, your wrists, anything else that happened to you while the Mayhem crew took you." Caius's voice is dripping with regret as he speaks. I suspect he thinks that he was too late and I was raped. I don't bother to correct him, though. I want him, and the rest of the Retribution Kings, to feel guilty for what they did.

"I owe you my life. Without your intervention, I would be dead," his voice softens. "I owe you a life, and I'll ensure that I repay my debt."

"You just saved my life. I think your debt has been repaid."

Caius shakes his head. "No, I didn't—"

He stops speaking when he looks up. I'm not sure what he's looking at, but I can feel a pair of eyes burning into my back.

Is it Beckett finally coming to check on me?

Slowly, I turn my head and find Lennox's jaw on the floor, his eyes wide as he stares at my back. Lennox hasn't been my biggest fan. I know he doesn't think I'm anything but trouble for their group. He doesn't trust me. His nostrils flare, and I think he's pissed at me for this, too, like I asked to be paraded around in a wedding dress then whipped into submission.

"What are you doing?" Lennox asks.

I scrunch my eyebrows, ready to fight this jerk, when Caius jumps up. "I needed to apologize to Ri for my part in this."

Lennox stomps toward us. "The best apology is to help her heal and reduce the pain right now. Then get revenge for what happened to her, understand?"

Caius nods, then he pats the bench. "Lie down on your stomach."

I want to get the dress off as soon as possible, but I doubt the guys have any clothes to change into that wouldn't cover the wound on my back. Instead, I decide to lie down on my stomach.

I hear Caius and Lennox cracking ice packs to activate them before placing them on my back.

I jump every time they place one on my back as pain initially shoots through me. But then I slump, relaxing into the bench as the cold starts numbing the pain.

"I need to get back to the helm. You know Gage can't

drive for shit, and if he lets Hayes take over, we'll end up driving toward the nearest party boat filled with half-naked women instead of heading toward the house," Lennox says.

Caius sits on the bench next to me, staring at me with guilt in his eyes. My eyes are closed, but I can feel his guilt pouring out of him.

"You can stop looking at me like that."

"No, I can't. This is all my fault. You wouldn't have had to endure any of that if my stupid ass hadn't gotten captured and needed rescuing."

I open my eyes. "My back and wrists will heal. We didn't finish the ceremony, and I didn't sign anything, so I'm not married. And..."

He stares at me intently.

"And other than smashing his lips against mine and palming my breasts, he didn't touch me. Everything he did I can heal from within a few days. So you can feel sorry about your part in deciding to drug me, tie me up, and scare me into talking to you guys, but don't blame yourself for me sacrificing myself to save you. That was my decision, not yours."

Caius hangs his head between his legs. I'm not sure if I got through to him, but I hope so. I can't stand watching him, or any man tear themselves up because they failed to protect me. They can call me Princess all they want, but I never asked to be one. I don't want to be a damsel in distress. I want to be able to protect myself.

"Why did you trade? Why did you save me?" he asks.

I stare at him, finally realizing that part of his shame comes from needing to be rescued. I feel the same. We both want to be strong, independent, and self-sufficient. We want to be able to save ourselves. Before Beckett, Caius was the leader of his crew. He wants to appear strong, not weak.

"I don't have a good answer for that. Maybe I thought it was the only way we were all getting out of there alive. Maybe I knew you'd all come to rescue me, and I wanted to prove to you guys that you couldn't threaten me while saving me. Maybe I was foolish enough to think that Paxton couldn't do anything to me that I couldn't endure."

"You're strong, Ri. One of the strongest people I've met, and I don't think I've seen the depth of your strength yet. I'm not even sure if you recognize your own strength. There is nothing you can't get through."

"I thought so, but being threatened by Paxton changed my perspective. There are definitely some things I'm not sure I'm strong enough to survive. Or at least things that will take a lot longer to heal from."

Caius stiffens, and I think he's going to promise to protect me from the things I can't survive. But he thinks better of it, because he wouldn't be able to keep his promise.

I try to clear my mind and think of something else when I realize that I've seen all of the guys except Beckett, and none of them have mentioned him. Is that one of the reasons all of the guys are so emotional—*Beckett didn't make it?*

My heart clenches at the thought of Beckett being injured or killed, but I have to know.

"Did Beckett...? Did Beckett make it?"

Caius frowns. "Beckett is meeting us at the cabin."

It's clear from what Caius isn't saying. Beckett didn't want to come save me. The rest of the guys went rogue and saved me on their own. I'm nothing to Beckett, not even an innocent girl worthy of his men's time to rescue. I deserved my fate.

I like the rest of the guys, and I know Beckett is married, but I thought we still shared some small connection. I thought he at least wanted me to help get Odette back. I thought we had a shot at being friends, if not allies, but now I know what Beckett and I really are—enemies.

14

BECKETT

I PACE back and forth in the cabin that serves as a safe house for the Retribution Kings. Even though the guys have accepted me as their leader, I'm not initiated yet, so Caius had to be the one to arrange the safe house with his father, who is technically still the leader. I never wanted to be a leader, but if it helps me get Odette back, I'll do whatever stupid initiation task it takes for me to have that power. And after I get Odette back, she and I will have a long talk about our future.

Unfortunately, that time will not be today. The lead Langston gave us brought us to a dead end. My heart lightens, knowing that she at least left the hotel alive. There's a chance she's still alive.

I glance at the clock on my phone; they should be back by now. Anxiety ripples through my body at all the different outcomes. Gage, Hayes, and Lennox should be relatively safe since the plan was for them to stay on the boat unless absolutely necessary to help in the rescue. Ri and Caius were most at risk, and any number of things could go wrong.

Yes, Ri has the best chance at giving me the information I need to get Odette back, but my anxiety is more than that. Ri doesn't deserve to die. Caius and the rest of the guys are slowly growing on me. I didn't grow up having much family.

I didn't even know my half-brother existed until recently. Even though I have a lot of friends I can call family now, these guys accepted me into their group immediately. They've been following orders and risking their lives to help me get my wife back. My responsibility is to keep them safe. And if I sent them on a mission that results in their deaths, I'm the one who has to take the blame and carry the guilt for the rest of my life.

It's not something I'm used to; I'd rather risk my own life. But I can't accomplish everything I need to by myself. I need their help. If this mission fails, it will just prove that my self-doubt is warranted.

I just hate waiting here doing nothing and hoping that everything turns out okay.

A low buzzing of an engine lifts my spirits—they're here.

I run out of the cabin and down through the woods toward the dock. The cabin is well hidden in the woods, and there is a small dock where the lake juts into the land, making the boat easy to hide from the lake as well. No one would know there is a cabin here unless they already knew of its existence.

The speedboat pulls into the small enclave as I stand on the dock, silently doing a headcount. One, two, three, four, five.

I let out a breath. They are all safe.

Lennox tosses me the rope, and I tie the boat up as it glides in. Lennox jumps onto the dock first, looking angry as usual. He nods his head at me then stomps toward the cabin without a word.

Gage climbs out next with a backpack full of electronics.

"The mission was successful?" I ask.

"Yes, but..." He glances back and then thinks better of whatever he was going to say. He pats my shoulder and then walks toward the cabin after Lennox. Hopefully, he'll get to work finding any other clues we've overlooked of who has Odette.

I turn my attention back to the boat. Even though I counted heads, I didn't get a good look at everyone's condition. Hayes stands in front of Ri and Caius—the ones I'm most concerned about.

Hayes jumps onto the dock and then turns to hold his hand out to Ri.

My mouth gapes at her. She's soaking wet as expected but wearing a fluffy white wedding dress and tiara on top of her still dripping dark hair. Her lips are tight, and her eyes seem to be throwing daggers at me as she takes Hayes's hand. I notice the wraps around her wrists—no doubt from the rope that I tied the previous day.

She steps barefoot onto the deck.

"Thank god, you're okay," I say.

Her eyes narrow her glare at me as she continues to hold Hayes's hand.

"Like you care," she snaps, continuing to walk with Hayes. "But yes, I'm okay as you put it."

They continue toward me, and I notice Caius is unharmed, just wet and shirtless as he hops off the boat looking concerned. I don't know why he's so anxious; the mission went off successfully.

But I follow his gaze to look at Ri and Hayes walking toward the cabin. It's then that I notice her back.

I gasp.

She whips her head around, daring me to say something. I know if I do, I'll get a smart comment back. But I'm speechless. Her back is covered in welts and slices through her beautiful skin. Blood still stains her back.

This is the fate we left her to. If they did this to her, there's no telling what else they did.

Caius walks toward me, and I grab his arm. "What happened?"

"They tried to whip her into submission. Tried to force her into marrying Paxton, their leader. She only agreed after he threatened my life." She's stronger than any of us realized.

"Did they hurt her? Other than her back, did he...?"

"No, she says no, but..."

I see the guilt in Caius's eyes. He blames himself for what happened to her, but that guilt is misplaced. I'm the one who deserves all the blame. It was my plan to take her to that field where we were attacked in the first place.

"Don't beat yourself up. It's my fault, not yours."

I release him and jog up the dock and through the woods to the cabin just as Hayes leads Ri inside. Caius enters just after me and goes to work securing the cabin with alarms and cameras.

"You need an Epsom salt bath and more pain killers. You'll feel better after a bath, and then we can put a compress on your back—"

Ri whips around at me, letting go of Hayes in the process who steps back. We are all standing in the living room. Lennox is enjoying the show. Gage is typing away on his laptop. Hayes is folding his arms and looking at me with an amused expression. And Caius is still entering codes into the panel next to the door.

"You don't get to tell me what to do! I get that all you care about is your wife. I'm nobody to you but a host of information and clues that could help you find her. But you could have at least come rescued me along with the guys. You shouldn't have left them to do your dirty work!"

"Actually—" Hayes steps in to correct her, but I glare at him, and he shuts up. It's better if she hates me.

"Are you finished?"

"No." She throws her tiara at me. "I'm not finished. I hate you! You left me to that—that...Ugh!" she screams at the top of her lungs.

Gage opens his mouth, no doubt to remind her that we are trying to remain quiet so no one knows we are here. I put my hand up, telling him to hush. She needs this.

I don't know what happened while she was captive, but it doesn't take much for me to piece together what she's upset about. I saw how she handles physical pain. Despite how ghastly her back looks, that's not why she's so upset. She was being forced to marry, no doubt knowing that he would rape her as soon as the vows were finished. That's what has her so rattled.

I'm not going to let Paxton win, though. Ri, despite her spoiled upbringing, is strong. She doesn't like to be seen as afraid, and she's going to need to keep her strength and spitfire in order to survive life with her father. If she continues on and the guys realize how afraid she is, she'll be embarrassed the next time she's around them.

She yells a second time, getting more of her emotions and fear out, but I can see the tears welling.

I stomp toward her.

"What are you doing?" She glares at me, her anger overtaking her fear.

Good, keep that anger at least until you are by yourself, then you can let loose, Princess.

Without another word, I scoop her up and throw her over my back.

"Beckett! Put me down!" She yells, her fists drilling into my back.

Hayes chuckles.

Lennox sneers.

Gage raises his eyebrows.

"Beckett, are you sure that's the best way to handle this?" Caius asks.

"Yep, I'm more than sure."

I stomp up the stairs to the master bedroom that will be hers while we stay here. The benefit of getting here early is that I had time to scope out the house.

I walk through the spacious master bedroom decorated in neutral grays and whites. It will be a perfect sanctuary for her to heal in. I head to the bathroom that has a large whirlpool tub.

I flip the warm water on with my foot. She's still yelling while beating against my back as I finally set her down.

"You're a fucking psychopath! Why do you think you have the power to tell me what to do? I'm not telling you a damn thing about what I know about Odette!"

I ignore her and dump Epsom salt into the bath that will help clean and soothe her back.

"Take a bath, Princess. I'll put some clothes for you just outside the door. When you're finished, you can kill me then."

And then I walk out of the bathroom before she has a chance to argue with me more. I shut the door and gather some clothes for her. As I set the clothes down, I hear her sobbing. I put my hand against the door, wishing I could comfort her.

If she didn't hate me, maybe I'd offer to, but that's not the kind of woman she is. She prefers to fall apart alone. So I leave her alone, hoping she's at least soaking in the bath, washing away any touch that vile man did to her.

I smell garlic and onions as I head downstairs and see that Hayes is in the kitchen cooking. I spot Gage on the couch still. Caius isn't in the main living space, so I suspect he's gone to shower and change clothes.

I head to the bar cart to start making drinks. I know Ri will want one, and I'm guessing the rest of the guys could use a drink as well.

Lennox approaches as I start pouring a bottle of bourbon into the first glass.

"I don't trust her," Lennox says.

I frown. "What are you talking about?"

"Princess—I don't trust her."

"What's there to trust? She sacrificed herself to save Caius. She took a whipping and didn't crack. I'm not saying she's on our side, but she's not against us."

"But that's the thing—why save Caius? Why go through what she suffered?"

I shake my head. "Drop it, Lennox. Leave Ri alone."

"I just think you are all thinking with your dicks instead of your brains."

"I'm not thinking with my dick."

"Sure you're not."

I punch him. How dare he think I would ever be disloyal to my wife.

Lennox dabs at the corner of his mouth. Blood drips

from the gash I just made in his lip. "I think I was wrong about you."

"What does that mean?" I ask.

"You'll make a better leader than I thought." Lennox walks back to the living room, and I go back to making drinks.

Caius jogs down the stairs and walks over to where I'm making drinks at the bar. He takes one and watches me closely as I pour more. "It's not my place, I'm not the one in charge anymore, but I think you should tell her."

"No."

"But—"

"No, I'm not telling Princess anything." Not when she keeps just as many or more secrets from me.

Caius sighs. "And the lead we had on Odette?" He swirls the single ice cube around in his drink, no longer meeting my eyes. I know losing Odette is just as hard on him as it is on me.

"Led to another dead end."

"But we know she's alive; that's better than before."

I nod, even though it doesn't mean a damn thing. Odette could be alive or long dead. All we know is she was alive when she was carried out of the hotel. What happened after, we have no clue. But like Caius, I need hope. I need to believe she's alive. It's the only thing keeping me from completely shattering.

Caius picks up another glass of bourbon and heads to the kitchen to hand one to Hayes. I take two glasses in my hand and hand them out to Lennox and Gage in the living room just as we hear footsteps descending down the stairs.

We all glance up in one motion as we watch Ri walking down the stairs barefoot. There is nothing covering her legs even though I put pajama pants out for her to wear.

My eyes continue up until they catch the hem of her white shirt that just covers her ass. Her nipples are hard against the thin material, and her dark hair is dripping down her front, making her shirt even more see-through.

I don't have to look at each of the guys to know they are drooling over her. If they didn't know about her injuries, it wouldn't surprise me to see them all try to get in her bed tonight.

"Snap out of it," I hiss at the room as I walk over to Ri. She's doing her best to hide her pain with every brush of the shirt against her back, but she can't help but wince.

I meet her at the base of the stairs. "Turn around."

She narrows her eyes. "Why?"

"So I can stop you moaning and causing every guy in this room's cock to twitch every time you do."

"Oh." She turns immediately.

I know my next actions aren't going to help the guys keep their dicks in their pants, but I'll worry about them. Ri should be comfortable.

Using my mouth and hand, I rip the back of her shirt open to expose her wounded back. I quickly inspect the stitches at her side and the wounds at her back for any signs of infection or needing restitching. At the moment, she seems like she's on the right track for healing.

"Turn."

She does, and then I tie the pieces from the back together around the front of her neck and ensure the shirt stays down below her breasts. Now her stomach and back are exposed, along with her black panties, but the shirt is no longer agitating the wounds on her back.

"Better?"

She nods but doesn't bother thanking me, not that I blame her.

She walks over to a spot on the sectional between Gage and Lennox. All four of their eyes stare intensely at her until I clear my throat.

I head to the hall closet and retrieve a throw blanket before grabbing a glass of bourbon and walking over to Ri.

"Bourbon, or would you like something else?"

She snatches the bourbon without speaking to me. She seems calmer, more collected than before, but it's clear that her anger for me hasn't diminished at all.

I toss the blanket on her legs. "In case you get cold," I say, instead of 'cover yourself up, so the guys stop making idiots of themselves.'

Caius and Hayes start bringing out bowls of pasta from the kitchen and handing them out to all of us. I sit on the edge of the fireplace to eat mine, while Caius and Hayes sit in the two remaining chairs.

"You made this, Heartbreaker?" Ri asks Hayes.

Hayes blushes at the nickname she gives him. "I've found that the ladies like a man who can cook, so I taught myself. And with you being Italian, I thought you would like a good carbonara."

"It's delicious," she beams at him.

He winks back at her.

I don't like their interaction at fucking all—not because I want her. Not because I know she's kissed at least three guys in this room, and it's going to start a war with the guys over her, but because there are strange feelings I feel about her—like I want to protect her.

I've never had a little sister, but I'm guessing this is what it feels like—to want the best for her and to not want to see her get hurt by some guy. I can't tell her who to date or fuck, and soon she's going to go back to her life with her family, but damn do I want to tell her to stop flirting with Hayes.

We all continue eating in relative silence. We've all had a long day. But I need answers.

I pull out my phone and walk over to Ri, kneeling in front of her. "Take a look at this video and see if you can identify anyone."

She reluctantly takes the phone and presses play on the grainy video of Odette being led out of the hotel through the back alleyway. There are two guys in the video, but both are wearing masks.

"Do you recognize anyone? Or the van she's being loaded in?"

"This is Odette?" Her eyes blink back tears.

I nod.

She exhales harshly, closing her eyes as she pushes the phone back into my hand. "I'm sorry, I don't know who those people are."

"Tell me what you know, Princess. What happened in that hotel?" My voice is harsher than I intended to, but I'm tired of waiting for answers.

Ri flinches.

Gage, who is closest, blocks me from touching her. "It's late, and we are all sleep-deprived. We aren't going to find Odette tonight. Let's reconvene in the morning when everyone has had a chance to cool down."

I growl. "I thought I was the one in charge."

Now, Hayes stands up. "We only have to listen to you when you finish initiation. Until then, anytime we follow you is just a courtesy."

I get in his face, but I notice all the men in the room are ready to fucking fight, and I'm guessing they'd all take his side, or in actuality, Ri's side.

"She's been through enough for tonight. You can talk tomorrow," Caius says, laying down the law.

I hate it. I hate all of it. I'm not giving up on you, Odette.

I decide that my time is best spent talking to my contacts and trying to get more information anyway, so I back down.

Ri shivers.

"You don't have to worry about anyone breaking in. This house is completely secure. There are cameras and motion sensors throughout the property. There is a gate you have to drive through to get here by land, and you saw how you can't see the house at all from the water. You're safe," Gage says.

"I know, thank you." She yawns again, ignoring the tension in the room. "I'm going to head to bed."

"You can have the room attached to the bathroom you bathed in. I'll be in the room next door. Caius is the next one. And Hayes will be in the third bedroom upstairs." I figure it's best to keep the guys who know her the best upstairs and close to her in case she needs anything. And I dictate where everyone is sleeping to try and take back control.

"Where are Gage and Lennox sleeping?"

"Couch city, Princess," Lennox says.

She frowns and shivers again. She's still rattled.

"I can sleep in your room on the floor if it would help? I'm pretty shaken up too, and I'd rather not sleep alone," Caius says.

"No, I'll sleep in your room, Caius, in your bed next to you," her eyes meet mine like this is some sort of retaliation.

But I'm not jealous. I'm not into her. I love my wife,

even if she lied to me and even if she doesn't love me back. *But then why do I care whose room she sleeps in?*

"That way Gage and Lennox can sleep in the king-sized bed instead of the couch," she continues.

She stands up, letting the blanket fall to the floor.

"Thanks, Princess." Gage grabs her hand and kisses the back of her hand.

Lennox just nods his thanks.

She walks past Hayes. "Sleep tight, Ri. If you can't handle Caius's snoring, there's always a spot open for you in my bed."

She rolls her eyes at him but can't help but smile. "Not going to happen, Heartbreaker."

And then she stops in front of Caius. "Take me to bed." She holds out her hand to him.

He takes it with a ridiculous grin.

They walk past me, and she doesn't so much as look at me. I hold back a growl. She hates me and thinks I hate her. Which is mostly true, but I'd stop hating her if she would just tell me how to get my wife back. And she'd stop hating me if I told her the truth.

I continue watching as they walk upstairs, not taking my eyes off them until they disappear beyond my sight.

"Sure, you're not thinking with your dick," Lennox says.

Gage snickers.

Hayes looks between us, confused. "What did I miss?"

"Nothing," I say.

"Just that Beckett finds Princess attractive and doesn't like Caius touching her," Gage says.

Hayes grins. "Of course he does. He's a hot-blooded man with eyes. Princess is fucking incredible. That's why so many men want her, not just because of the power that comes from her father."

"I don't want Ri. I'm married. I love Odette, even if..." I shake my head. "Ri means nothing to me."

"We're not saying you are going to cheat on your wife. Or that you love Ri; it's just lust. But if you would recognize the spark between you two, then maybe you'd realize why you both almost burn the house down every time you are in the same room together," Lennox says.

"She's just a means to an end. And any spark you see between us is just mutual hatred."

Gage laughs. "You forget that, unlike Ri, we know the truth. We know who arranged to rescue her. We know what you did."

"Enough. Go to bed and get some sleep. And no more fighting my orders if you know what's good for you. Tomorrow we are going to find Odette."

"And what about Ri?" Hayes asks.

"Don't get attached." I know how her story ends—with us returning her to her father and begging for forgiveness.

15

RI

CAIUS HOLDS the door open to his bedroom, releasing my hand and allowing me to walk in front of him. He follows me but at a distance as I enter the large room. There's a king bed, two nightstands, and a TV mounted on a pale blue wall.

Caius stands at the door, studying me closely, probably for signs I'm about to crack.

"I can leave the door open if that will make you more comfortable?"

I smile at him and shake my head.

Slowly, he closes the door, his hand hovering over the lock until I nod. Only then does he lock it. There's a reason I chose to sleep in his room. I feel safe around him.

Hayes is flirtatious and a good kisser, but he's too reckless. Lennox hates my guts. I haven't gotten to know Gage well enough to trust him. And Beckett would probably stab me in my sleep if it meant I'd tell him where his wife is. Caius is the only one I trust.

"You can have the bathroom first," Caius says.

I nod again and head into the bathroom. I quickly pee

and find a new toothbrush in the drawer to brush my teeth with. Then I sit on one side of the bed while Caius takes his turn in the bathroom.

He reemerges shirtless, but he's left his joggers on.

"I can sleep on the floor," he offers, running his hand through his hair so I get a good view of his biceps and chest flexing.

I bite my lip. "Don't be ridiculous. It's a king-sized bed. I'm sure we can find a way to share it." I pat the bed next to me.

With a tense smile, Caius eases himself down onto the bed next to me.

"Do you happen to be a stomach sleeper?" he asks.

I frown. "I'm the tossing and turning type."

He nods, picking at his nails as he considers his next words.

"You're too sweet, you know that?"

He chuckles. "I'm not sweet. I wish I was, but the things I've done aren't sweet."

"You're sweet to me." I put my hand on his, getting small tingles through my arm when I touch him. We share a spark. It's not as intense as the one I feel around Beckett, but maybe that's because I don't want to murder Caius in his sleep like I do with Beckett. My emotions are more intense with Beckett because hate is stronger than like. I like Caius; I hate Beckett. My feelings for Caius could grow.

I withdraw my hand suddenly as I realize who I am and what my role is. I don't get to choose my future, not until I find a way to truly escape. Anything that would happen between me and these guys would just be a fling with no feelings and no future. Caius is too sweet to hurt that way. I don't take him as a one-night stand kind of guy.

He's too caring for that. Plus, my father would kill him if Caius fucked me.

"So Hayes gets a nickname...do you have a nickname for me?" His cheeks pink as he asks.

My eyes glow with mischief as I pretend to think about it. "Sweetheart?"

He scrunches his nose.

"Sweetie pie?"

His frown darkens.

"Sweet cheeks?"

"I'll think I'll settle for no nickname until you can come up with something more manly."

I chuckle, rolling my eyes. These guys are easy to make jealous.

"Do you want to talk?" he asks.

I run my hands through my hair, rocking forward in the bed. "I'm confused because that's what I thought we've been doing this whole time."

He grins. "I meant about what you went through? What you're feeling?"

I shake my head.

"Or what you know about where Odette might be or who might have her?"

Our eyes meet, and all that's shining back at me is deep pain in his blue eyes.

"You may hate Beckett and not want him to get his wife back, but she's my sister, my best friend. We were born less than a year apart. We were close—no, we are close. I want my sister back. If you won't talk to Beckett, talk to me."

"I'll talk to Beckett tomorrow. I'll tell him everything I know. I can't go back. I need him to promise to help me get free."

"I can help you..."

"You can't. You aren't in charge, not anymore. He is, so it's him I should talk to." I place my hand on his shoulder. "If my father has her, he won't hurt her. He wants me back too much, and he knows the only way to do that is by keeping her alive so Beckett will trade." But if my father doesn't have her, then I have no clue what's happened to Odette. She could be dead.

He places his hand on top of my mine and squeezes his thanks.

I gently turn and lay onto my stomach, gripping the pillow under my head as I stare up at him. "Tell me about her."

"Odette?" He pushes himself down until he's lying on his side facing me.

I nod, trying to look at his eyes and not his contracting muscles, but it's damn hard.

"Odette is technically ten months older than me, but I've always thought of her as an annoying little sister. She was shorter, smaller than me, and I was very protective of her. When we were little, she was always trying to get me to play dress up and painted my face with her makeup. As we got older and she started dating, I was the one who'd beat up the guys who broke her heart. But if you think I'm sweet, just wait until you meet Odette." His face lights up as he speaks about her.

"Odette is the kind of person who always holds the door open for others, gives every last penny she saves to charity, volunteers at the soup kitchen on her days off, and ensures every stray animal she finds on the street gets a good home."

"Sounds like someone else I know, Charming."

"Charming? I like it." He lights up.

I yawn again. "Tell me more."

Caius climbs out of bed and turns off the lights before he tells me more stories about Odette as I drift off to sleep.

———

I wake up before the sun, but there is no use trying to fall asleep again. My back burns, and I need painkillers to ease the pain.

Caius is snoring loudly next to me. His hand is draped over my back, which is I'm sure what woke me up. I roll out from under his arm as a shiver runs through me. I pick up his joggers that he must have ditched at some point in the night and slip them on, but don't add any layers to my top half. My back and side still hurts too much for that. Then I head out in search of coffee.

The kitchen has a Keurig machine. I wrinkle my nose, knowing it won't make the best cup of coffee and hating that the pods are horrible for the environment, but I need coffee, so this will have to do.

I dig through the cabinet for a cup and put a pod in and press the button. The delicious smell of coffee being made immediately hits my nose, and I smile.

I grab my mug of coffee, deciding I should go sit out on the back deck to watch the sunrise. I stumble outside and see the outline of someone already sitting in the first chair.

I tilt my head, and then I get a glimpse of who's sitting here. "Gage?"

"Hey, Princess. I didn't expect you to be up this early."

"Couldn't sleep with Caius's snoring."

Gage chuckles but then frowns when I wince.

"Could it also have to do with the fact that your back hurts like a bitch?"

"That might have something to do with it."

"One second." Gage jogs back into the house and returns with a bottle of pills. I hold out my hand, and he dumps a couple into my palm. I throw them back in my mouth.

"Thanks."

I go back to sipping my coffee, and I notice Gage has one as well. "You an early riser, or is there a reason you are up this early?"

He sighs. "Just trying to figure out what I missed, why we can't figure out who took Odette. It doesn't make sense. There should be more clues as to where she went."

"You stayed up all night looking for her?"

"That, and I kept an eye on the security system to keep us safe."

"How can I help?"

Gage's eyebrows shoot up. He grabs his laptop and fires it up. "You can tell me any locations where your father might keep Odette."

My face drops. "My father—he didn't exactly keep me informed of his criminal activities. He barely talked to me; I barely knew him, but..."

I stare at the map Gage has pulled up of the city, considering.

"But?" Beckett asks, stepping out of the darkness.

I nearly jump out of my skin. "Have you been there the whole time?"

"Yes."

"Why didn't you tell me you were there?"

He cocks his head. "I didn't know that I needed to announce my presence."

"You wanted to spy on me."

"Maybe." He shrugs.

Insufferable.

I down the rest of my coffee, knowing it's time that Beckett and I have a conversation. I stand up from my chair. "Let's talk."

Beckett stiffens and then starts walking without a word.

I follow after and realize we are walking down to the dock. Beckett sits on the edge, his feet hanging over the water. I sit next to him, doing the same.

The sun is just beginning to rise finally, and his face glows in the early morning light.

"So our deal—you ready to accept?" he asks.

"Our deal for you to help me escape my father in exchange for information that can help you get Odette back?"

"Yes, that deal. Although based on listening to you talk to Gage, I doubt you have information that can help us."

"I do, actually," I snap back.

"Then, I'm all ears."

"How do I know I can trust you? That you won't use me as a bargaining chip to get Odette back?"

"You don't."

I frown. "Not really helping me to want to tell you anything."

"I'm offering you a deal, but there are other ways I could get you to talk."

"Asshole."

"You're not wrong."

I sigh. I'm not sure if I believe him when he offers to help me. But then again, the information I have might not even lead to him finding Odette. My father may not have her. But after listening to Caius all last night, I want to help. Caius deserves to have his sister back even if Beckett doesn't deserve to have his wife back.

I hold out my left hand to him.

He cautiously takes it.

"Deal."

We shake.

"Tell me everything you know. Tell me if you think your father took her. Tell me why. Tell me where he might have taken her. Tell me the best way to get her back."

I nod and close my eyes, taking a deep breath to decide where to start. But nothing comes to me. I draw a blank space.

I think harder about my past, about which details to share, but every detail I've ever thought vanishes. I can't remember who I was running from or why. I can't remember where I went to school. I can't remember my family, my friends, birthdays, special occasions, afternoon coffees—all of it gone.

The images that do appear are foggy shadows, like ghosts haunting me.

Why can't I remember?

Have I been drugged so much lately that I'm having temporary amnesia?

That must be it, but that doesn't help Beckett find Odette. If I can't tell him anything, then he'll trade me back to my father, which is the one thing I don't want. I feel that deep in my gut.

More importantly, I have a new intense terror. I don't know who I am. I don't remember my past. In an instant, it feels like everything was taken from me.

I stare at Beckett as panic consumes me. "I'm sorry."

He frowns. "Ri?"

And then I jump up and run toward the house. I run from Beckett. I run from my fear.

But in a second, both have caught up to me.

BECKETT

"Rɪ?!"

She jumps up and starts running down the dock away from me.

What the hell?

I thought we finally had a breakthrough. I thought she was ready to talk. I was sure after spending the night with Caius that his good heart and stories of Odette would have softened her. Once she knew it wasn't just me that missed Odette, I thought Ri would want to make a deal with me.

What changed her mind?

I start running after her while searching for any signs of someone who might have spooked Ri, but I don't hear or see anyone.

"Ri!" I shout as I catch up to her.

She stops and turns to face me like she doesn't even know what she's doing.

"What's going on? What happened back there?" I point over my shoulder with my thumb, completely not following her actions.

She purses her lips as her chest rises and falls hard like she just ran a marathon instead of fifty feet.

I feel my rage rising, but I push it back down. I have to be gentle with her.

"Tell me what's going on...please," my voice breaks when I say please. Every second that Odette is gone is another second I might not get her back. As much as I'm not sure where my relationship with Odette stands, I know one thing hasn't changed—I love her. I can't lose her.

Ri looks at the fear of losing Odette in my eyes, and I see tears in her own. I reach my hand out to her. She takes it without thinking. This is it—the moment when she finally tells me.

But she doesn't speak. She just gasps like there isn't enough oxygen in the world.

"I'll protect you from your father. I'll protect you from everyone. I'll owe you the rest of my life if you help me get Odette back. I'll kill for you. I'll make sure you're safe, forever." This time I mean my promise.

Ri opens her mouth, and I nod my head, encouraging her to speak. She glances down at our hands, and in that moment, something changes. She releases my hand.

"I'm sorry." Once again, she's running.

"Dammit." I run after her.

I expect her to dart into the woods, to try to find a way to escape, but instead, she heads back into the cabin. *Maybe she thinks Caius or one of the other guys will help her like they did before?*

I chase her inside, and Ri stops suddenly in the living room. She seems to have no idea what her next move is, just that she has to get away from me.

I'm not letting her get away again. I'm tired of games.

I jump, tackling her onto the couch.

"What are you doing?! Get off of me!" Ri shouts, wiggling beneath me as I fight to pin her hands over her head. Finally, I succeed.

She snarls at me.

"There she is. I thought Ri left and a ghost must have entered your body, but there's the fight I expect. I thought we could do this in a civilized way with a mutual agreement that works for both of us. But if you prefer the hard way, that's fine with me."

She tries to buck me off of her while trying to get her wrists out of my grasp, but I'm not letting her go until she tells me what she knows.

"You know something. Were you in on the plan to kidnap Odette? Is that why you're afraid?"

"Go to hell!"

"Tell me where Odette is!" I growl.

She looks at me with defiance. Finally, I realize what I've refused to believe this entire time. Ri won't tell me anything with gentle persuasion, not to save her own life, not to avoid torture.

This isn't the way. I have to find another.

I need to find out if she loves someone I can threaten. Or I need to figure out how to get her father to make a trade with me.

I grip her wrists harder, and my body pushes harder into hers until I know her back is crushing into the couch.

She winces only slightly.

"Do you hate your father?"

She frowns.

"Answer me." I jerk into her body.

"Yes, I hate my father."

"Why?"

"He's a cruel man."

I nod. "But you're not. Tell me..." my lips linger over hers, trying everything possible to get her to tell me how to save my wife.

She licks her lips and continues to breathe harder, her throat tightening as she swallows. My body hardens over hers, but it must be because I'm incredibly angry. I'm fucking furious; this is my body's response. I'm not attracted to her.

"I can't. I'm sorry," she says.

"I'll blame you if anything happens to Odette."

I release her wrists and begin to ease off of her.

I hear some of the guys walking in behind me.

"Lennox is right. You are hiding something. I'm going to figure out what it is."

I stand up.

Ri doesn't move, not even to ease the sting of her back.

I start to walk away but stop.

"I truly thought you would tell me. I thought you were a better person than me, than your father, than all of us. Turns out I should have been calling you Devil instead of Princess all along."

I glance to my right and see Caius standing, wanting to jump in but unsure of what to do. I look back to Ri. "Talk to Caius if you want to live, and if you don't want me to figure out what you're hiding. You have until I get back if you don't want me to turn you over to your father."

Then I force myself to leave the room before I kill her and lose the only lead I have.

17

RI

I TREMBLE WATCHING Beckett walk out of the room. I feel the other guys' gazes on me as I shake. I run my hand down my face feeling sweat on my brow. My entire body is raging hot—my core aching with fiery desire or maybe searing anger. I can't decide if I want to go after Beckett to jump his bones or murder him.

I decide I'd regret either decision as I sit up on the couch in a daze. Caius is moving toward me, and I'm pretty sure Lennox and Hayes are also staring, but I don't look at any of them. Despite the intense moment I just had with Beckett, I need time to figure my own shit out.

I run upstairs wordlessly, my mind barely working.

"Ri!" Caius shouts after me.

I ignore him and keep running up the stairs. I consider turning into Caius's room where I slept last night, but instead, I head into the master. I slam the door just as Caius reaches the top step. I turn the lock and stare at the door, waiting for him to break it down.

After a few seconds, I remember Caius isn't Beckett and realize he's not going to break the door down. I sigh and turn to the room, not sure what I should do next. I run my hand through my long hair, parting it to one side. I close my eyes and beg my brain to remember, but I draw a blank. There isn't even a tingling of a memory before I met Beckett.

That can't be a coincidence, can it?

What happened to me? It had to be the drugs. How else would I have lost all my memories?

I consider heading back out and telling them the truth. I can't remember, that's why I can't help them. Caius might believe me, but Beckett wouldn't. He'd try to torture it out of me. I'm surprised he hasn't already. Maybe Beckett didn't think I was worth his time, and he went to find his wife on his own. The only good I am to him now is a bartering chip with my father. He's going to send me back.

No, I have to get out of here. I always knew I couldn't stay. These guys don't actually care about me, not even Caius. He's trying to get me to spill as much as Beckett is; both of them would do anything to get Odette back. And the other guys will do whatever Caius and Beckett say.

I could try lying to them, but I wouldn't even know how to fake giving them information.

My only chance at surviving is if I can escape now before Beckett strikes a deal with my father to exchange me for Odette. After I'm free, I can figure out what the hell is fucked up with me.

I head into the closet and pull out a pair of jeans, a tank top, and a leather jacket. I start getting dressed and realize the clothes are maybe a size too small, but I manage to squeeze into them. I slip on some heeled boots that are actually my size. I'd be better off with tennis shoes for running, but there are none that fit in the closet.

Getting dressed was the easy part. Now I have to figure out how to get out of here without being noticed.

I wait until the middle of the night to sneak out, or what I hope is the middle of the night. There is no clock in the room, but it's been dark for several hours, and I don't hear anyone moving in the house, so hopefully, everyone is asleep.

I push the bedroom door open and listen, still nothing. I head down the stairs, careful to not make a sound. One of the men snores softly on the couch—Gage, I realize. I tiptoe past him. Then, I head toward the garage. I flick the lights on and let out a sigh.

There are two cars in the garage. I pick what looks like the fastest and open the door. It takes me a full two seconds to realize the key is already in the ignition. I pop open the center console and find a burner phone, a wad of cash, and credit cards.

I grin.

Thank god they needed a quick getaway car and kept everything needed to escape in the cars. I hit the garage door open, and then I floor it, hoping none of the guys are light sleepers.

The road is rocky, but I make it, only to find a large iron gate about a mile down the road.

Shit.

I look around the center console, the visor, the seat next to me, anywhere a button could be that would open the gate. But I can't find anything.

Fuck, fuck, fuck. I hit the steering wheel over and over. If I have to go on foot, I won't make it through the night before the guys catch me.

But as I slow in front of the gate, it starts to swing open

automatically. I gun it as soon as a wide enough gap appears.

My heart beats wildly as I drive this incredibly fast, expensive car. I need to head into the city to find a train or plane to take me out of here. I'm sure this car has some sort of tracking device on it, so I need to ditch it as soon as possible.

I find the main road and drive almost an hour to get back to the city. I park the car on a random sidestreet and climb out, running my hand over the hood of the car. Apparently, I'm a car girl. I leave the keys in the car, hoping it gets stolen. It would just lead the guys on a wild goose chase and give me more time to run.

I walk five blocks to the nearest subway station, ride for eight stops, and climb off quickly. I don't know where I am, but that's kind of the point.

It's close to midnight as I walk down the street, but it's a weekend, so Chicago is still very much alive. I consider my options. I could find a hotel room, but I don't want to waste my cash on anything but a flight out of here. Instead, I decide to wait in a bar for a couple of hours before heading to the airport and catching the first flight out in the morning. I duck into a nightclub with a group of women, without having to flash an ID.

Lights blind me as music pulses through my body. I don't bother to take in much of my surroundings. It's crowded and unlikely that I'll be found by anyone. I can drown my sorrows and think through my plan.

"Cheapest beer you have," I say, slapping a five down on the bar.

The bartender nods at me stiffly, taking my five and returning with a bottle a moment later. He pops the top off and slides it to me. I tilt it back, not caring what it is.

As I drink, someone bumps into me.

I wince.

I forgot until now that my back and side are still sore. Earlier, all I could feel was Beckett. Now, reality is setting in again. I'm on the run for my life from multiple dangerous men with a shredded back, stitches barely holding me together, no memory, maybe five hundred dollars, a burner phone, and the clothes on my back. I'm totally screwed.

I down the beer, and the bartender immediately brings me another. I get to my third beer before something changes. I feel the shift in the air and intense stares without turning around.

"Where's the tracker?" I ask when Caius sits down on the stool on my left, Hayes on my right, Lennox and Gage behind me.

"Now, why would we tell you that, Princess?" Hayes asks, waving down the bartender and getting everyone a round of beers.

I continue to stare straight ahead as I sip my beer, thinking of where it could be.

"You shoved it down my throat when you drugged me," I conclude, realizing I have no scars unaccounted for and I'm not wearing any jewelry they could be tracking.

"Definitely not just a pretty face," Gage says from behind me.

I shoot daggers back.

"You can't run from us, Princess," Caius says.

"I don't really have another option, Charming."

"You could talk to us. We can help you, but only if you help us find Odette. She's my sister. I love her." Caius puts his finger under my chin and turns my head toward him, so I can see his emotional plea.

"Please, Ri, I'm lost without her. And I don't want to hurt you, but I will. We all will, to get her back."

I feel tension oozing from the guys. They are each furious with me in their own way. Lennox has pure hatred that I've never been worth saving. Gage is annoyed that I slipped through his security. Hayes is frustrated that he has to torture me, which will ruin his shot at getting to fuck me. And Caius is hurt that I won't help him find his sister. None of their emotions make me spill the truth any faster.

"Ri, please," Caius says as I feel the guys moving in. They have a plan, and I'm sure the cuts on my back will be nothing compared to what they do to me.

"I can't."

"Yes, you can, just tell us. No one wants to torture you," Hayes says, turning me toward him.

Lennox grunts.

"Okay, maybe Knox does a bit. But he's just fucked up in the head, that's all," Hayes grins at his friend.

"No, I mean, I literally can't tell you, not that I won't."

Hayes cocks his head. "I'm not sure what you mean."

"I mean, I can't remember."

Caius grabs my face then, drawing me back to him and his musky scent. "Talk to me, Princess. What do you mean you can't remember? You can't remember the night that Odette went missing?"

I shake my head. "I mean, I can't remember any of it. That night, my childhood, my teenage years—nothing before being covered in blood and running into Beckett in the hotel lobby that night—long after whatever happened to Odette happened." Tears start flowing—for myself, for Odette, for this whole fucked up situation.

Caius's eyes drift up, and he silently exchanges conversations with all the guys.

"Do you believe me?" I ask.

"We believe you."

"Even you, Len?"

Lennox frowns. "I believe you're scared, Princess, and it's not of us." He flicks my ear, trying to prove that I am, in fact, scared of them. I refuse to shiver like he wants, though.

"Why can't I remember?" I ask, hoping one of the guys has an idea or will admit that it's a side effect of the drugs they gave me.

Gage drinks his beer, ignoring my stare. Lennox shrugs like he doesn't really care. Hayes taps the bottom of his beer bottle. And Caius freezes with his eyes dazed.

"Thanks for the help, guys. I really appreciate it," I say snarkily.

"Why didn't you tell Beckett?" Gage asks.

I look up at him. "He wouldn't believe me if I did."

Gage frowns and then nods his head, agreeing, as he sips his beer. Music blares around us with people dancing and drinking, carrying on not knowing that this is a crossroads in my life. What happens next will change the course of everything.

The guys now believe I have no information to help them, so there is no reason to torture me, but they can't just let me go either. They want Odette, not me. They still think my father is likely the one who took her, and if he didn't, he's the most powerful man in the city. He could figure out where she is in a heartbeat for them.

They only have one option—trade me to my father for Odette or for information they need to find her.

These guys were never my friends. Any kindness they

showed was to manipulate me into talking. Now they're going to screw me over, and honestly, I want them to. I'm not a monster. An innocent woman shouldn't die. My life was always destined to end this way. No amount of running would save me.

But maybe something else could save me...

"Fuck me, Caius."

"Wait...what?" He blinks rapidly like he doesn't think he heard me correctly.

"You're going to return me to my father to get Odette back. I understand, but fuck me first."

Caius tilts his head, his eyebrow raising. "I don't understand how that would help anything."

I turn to face Hayes. "Fuck me, Heartbreaker."

"My pleasure, Princess." Hayes takes my hand and kisses it.

"Wait," Caius grabs my other hand and turns me toward him.

I smirk.

"Why?" Caius asks again, glaring at where Hayes is still gripping my hand.

"My father wants to marry off his virgin daughter to the highest bidder. I've known of my fate since I was thirteen. It's a miracle I've managed to stay free this long. I can't change the arranged marriage part, but I can piss him off by losing my virginity, limiting the guys he can sell me to."

"You're really a virgin?" Caius asks.

I shrug. "I don't know, I don't remember. But I know one thing—I won't be one when I go back to my father."

"If Caius fucks you, he'll be signing his death warrant. Corsi won't let him live. The rest of those motherfuckers thought if they fucked you or married you, your father would honor it, but all he would have done is kill them. Caius can't fuck you, Princess," Gage says.

I give him a tight smile. He's the honest, practical one and his words make sense. As much as I want to piss off my father and possibly save myself for a bit longer, I don't want to do it if it risks their lives.

I finish my beer. "Take me to my father tonight. You shouldn't wait any longer, not when Odette's life is on the line."

None of the guys speak immediately. I assume they are letting me drown in my sorrows, or maybe buying me a harder drink before they take me. Or maybe they're calling Beckett to let him know about their plan.

Lennox and Gage walk away; Gage with his phone to his ear, probably arranging the meeting. I slump into my seat.

"Trust us, Princess. We're the Retribution Kings; we don't get revenge unless it's deserved," Caius whispers against my ear.

"And we're about to get revenge for you against your father," Hayes whispers in the other.

I have no idea what either of them are talking about, how they can help, or why, but Hayes holds out his hand to me. His wicked eyes warn me that if I take his hand, there is no going back.

I may not know who I used to be, but the woman I am now doesn't back down from a challenge. I put my hand in Hayes's—challenge accepted. I just don't have a clue what I'm saying yes to.

18

RI

HAYES LEADS me through the club to a backroom. He kisses the back of my hand and winks at me before leaving me alone in the room and walking out.

My heart thumps in my chest as I wait for him or one of the guys to reenter and tell me what's going on. But minutes tick by, and no one enters.

I put my hand on the doorknob; it doesn't turn. I'm locked in.

I glance around the room. It has several couches, a pool table, a dartboard, a stripper pole, and a small bar in the corner. It must be used as a private party room.

I walk over to one of the couches and lie down as I yawn. I might as well make the most of my time and take a nap while I wait for the guys to return.

A loud slam of the door wakes me. I jolt up, expecting to see the guys, but instead find the lights flickering and a dozen guys with devil masks.

I rub my eyes, thinking I must be dreaming, but the men all continue to stalk toward me. I realize this is very real, and I'm in very real threat of dying.

Music booms through the room, and the club lights continue to strobe, making it impossible for me to see everything. I don't know exactly how many guys are approaching me, but it's too many for me to escape from. I grab for the pillows behind me, thrusting one in front of me like it is somehow going to protect me.

Fuck, what are the odds of another gang coming after me? Did my father put out a reward or something to find me?

"What do you want?" I ask, but they don't answer me. They just stalk toward me like a group of lions circling their prey.

"The Retribution Kings are here. They'll kill you if you touch me," I say, hoping my warning is enough to back them off.

"They'll have to catch us first," a deep voice growls into my ear as he grabs my shoulders.

I dig my nails into his hands, trying to fight him off as two more guys lunge at me. I kick wildly and scream for help, trying to keep the guys from advancing long enough that someone can hear me and come to my rescue.

The music is too loud for anyone to hear, though. One of the guys catches my boot in his hand. Another grabs my other foot. I'm defenseless. My only hope is that the Retribution Kings still want to rescue me again, knowing that I have no information to help them. Hopefully, my value as a trade commodity is enough for them to come to my rescue.

I continue to struggle in the guys' arms, expecting them to tie my arms behind my back, drug me into unconsciousness, and drag my lifeless body out of here and into a car. What I don't expect is the removal of my clothes. My jacket goes first, then my shoes. Then a hand pushes underneath my shirt, palming my breast.

I freeze.

These men are going to rape me. *What do I do? How do I save myself?*

"Don't act like you won't enjoy this, Princess," heady words are whispered into my ears.

Princess.

The club lights flash again, and I see a camera set up in the corner of the room. I count the men—one, two, three, four. Not a dozen. I look at the shirtless men and study the tattoos on two of the torsos.

It all happens in a split second. My brain processes what's happening. These guys aren't strangers coming to kidnap me; these are the Retribution Kings fulfilling their promise to save me.

A smile lifts before I realize there is a reason they didn't tell me. They wanted my real reaction. They wanted me to show fear so my father couldn't blame me for losing my virginity. The guys are wearing masks, so they can't be identified. And they are all going to participate, so if they are somehow identified, they'll all take the blame.

I told them earlier I'd be willing to fuck them all. They know I want this. They know I'll enjoy this. But it doesn't stop my heart from racing to terrifying speeds.

Can I really handle this? Four guys at once?

I'm about to find out.

Caius starts lowering a blindfold over my eyes.

No, I want to see. My mind will play tricks on me if I can't see. But Caius's stern eyes through his mask say I don't have a choice—being a little terrified is a good thing.

I take a deep breath and surrender as the blindfold goes over my face. But I can't hold back my scream as my jeans are shredded from my body.

A maddening chuckle rings out around me. These fuckers are enjoying my fear.

My body is lifted up off the couch, and I'm carried by my legs and arms. I land on a hard surface—I'm guessing the pool table.

I fight as I feel my arms being lifted over my head and my legs being spread. I scream some more, enjoying the thrill now that I know who's doing the scaring. We haven't even gotten to the enjoyable part yet.

The fear should be gone now, but it's not. My titillation grows stronger every second, not knowing what to expect. *What are they going to do to me? Am I going to like it, enjoy it, crave it? Are they going to push my limits too far? Is this the right thing to save me from my father, or am I only going to provoke him?*

None of it matters—I want this. For once, I'm doing something for myself. I don't know if I'm a virgin or not. I don't know who I'll be forced to marry or if I'll find a way to escape. What I do know is that even though I have four beasts holding onto my limbs, this is my decision. This is me taking control and them fulfilling my fantasy.

I'm guessing this is how Caius is paying me back for saving his life.

My tank, bra, and underwear are still on as my arms are held above my head and my legs spread. I hiss as a thumb rubs harshly over the bandage on my wrist.

"Sorry, Princess," someone leans in and whispers. I don't know why I can't identify who he is by his voice. His lips press against mine upside down. I can't match the kiss to Hayes's or Caius's previous kisses, just that his tongue slips in, swirling around and setting my body on fire.

I don't know why none of the other guys have touched me yet except to spread me on the pool table. I'm guessing that while they may want it to look like they're hurting me, they don't actually want to hurt me. They want it to feel good, and they're giving me another chance to stop it.

They plan on being gentle while pretending to fuck me hard. *Not going to happen.*

I bite down on my kisser's top lip. He groans and jerks my wrists tighter, causing me to bite harder.

He must signal to the group because that's when I finally feel their hands starting. A hand rips my tank from my body, shredding it until my stomach and back are bare, and I can feel felt scratching against the scars on my back. Nails claw down my smooth stomach, and I suck in my stomach as fingers glide over my panties.

I buck my hips, wanting more than just rough nails.

"Be careful what you beg for, Princess," another voice whispers in my ear. A hand reaches behind my back, undoes my bra, and removes it from my body. I fight for the fun of it as the men work the bra off my arms.

"Play nice, Princess."

"Never," I defy.

Another set of lips takes over my mouth, kissing me so hard that I forget to breathe. His tongue dips in and out of my mouth, giving me no time to react when I feel another's hands pinch my nipples.

"Jesus Christ," I curse.

A loud hackle howls through the room at my reaction to the simple touch.

"Somebody isn't used to being touched. Just wait until we're through with you. We are going to ruin you for every other man."

I have no doubt they will. I can't imagine a hotter experience.

A tongue licks down a sensitive spot on my neck as a mouth encases my nipple.

I moan as the tongue swirls over my sensitive bud—flicking and sucking and working me so that my entire body is electric. I'm pretty sure I could come just from whatever his tongue is doing to my nipple alone.

Lips land back on my mouth, lips I think belong to Hayes, and I feel another pair kissing up my legs.

I freeze—not that I have much movement—but every hair on my body stands up as the man between my legs roughly kisses up my inner thigh. My legs are still pulled apart, my feet flat on the felt table with my knees spread, fully exposed to the man between them. The only thing blocking his view is my black cotton panty underwear.

For a moment, I let my thoughts drift to what the guys must be thinking. *Do they find me attractive even though I'm not wearing lingerie? Even though I'm not experienced? Even though they don't care about me?*

My thoughts are just a distraction from the guy inching closer to my sex.

Am I really doing this? Am I really going to let them fuck me—all four of them?

The man gently kisses over my panties, and I suck in a breath, still not completely sure if I'm going to go through with this. I'm brave and smart, *but can I really do this?*

"Awww," I half growl and scream as I feel teeth nipping my sensitive clit through my underwear. The heat that spreads is like nothing else. Lust consumes me. If I hadn't already forgotten all of my memories, I would in this moment. I can't turn back. I need to feel him and every other man in this room inside me. I need them to fill me, to fuck me.

I feel his smirk over my underwear, knowing he was

the one that convinced me. I'm a depraved soul who needs to be fucked by four men in order to be saved.

My panties are ripped from my body, and then I'm naked in front of them. Despite music filling our ears, I can still hear their heavy breathing. The fact that I don't feel anyone kissing, licking, or nipping at me anymore tells me they have all stopped to stare at my naked body.

I try to curl away, slightly embarrassed that I'm completely naked in front of four gods. But the arms holding me in place don't let me.

"You're beautiful, Princess."

"Maybe we should start calling you Goddess?"

"Our sexy Princess."

"Slutty is more like it."

I hear all their comments whisper over my skin. And then it's all of their lips finding a different piece of my skin to worship. My thigh, my stomach, my neck, my lips—all sensitive areas, but nowhere I really want them to kiss.

"Please," I cry. I should be careful with my words if I don't want my father to think I agreed to this depravity, but my please could easily be mistaken for a cry to let me go instead of a plea to fuck me.

Chuckles ring out around the room, and then they give me what I beg for. Hands descend on my breasts while lips suck my nipples hard. Harsh lips devour my mouth. But the fingers dancing over my clit are what have my toes curling.

A thumb brushes over my clit, and I jolt at how intense it feels. I simultaneously feel lips smirking at my mouth and nipple, laughing at my reaction.

I've got to hold it together. If I react this strongly to a thumb brushing over my clit, I'm never going to survive the intense feeling of them all fucking me.

Then the man between my legs does something fucking incredible. His mouth presses over my sex, and his tongue finds my clit, flicking and sucking it.

My back arches, my hips drive up, and the damn scream that leaves my throat vibrates through the entire room.

"Holy shit!" I curse. *It's so much.*

It has to be Caius between my legs. No other man would worship me so and want me to feel this good before he fucks me.

I still can't see anything with the blindfold, and I'm beginning to think that's a good thing. I don't think I could handle how intense I'm feeling while watching them. I'd be too self-conscious.

"You're so wet, Princess. I can see how wet you are from here," is whispered into my ear.

I moan and squirm while they continue to pin me to the table.

"Come, Princess, come all over my tongue." The tongue flicks into me as a thumb presses over my clit, and I come. It ripples through my body, starting at my core and then bursting out of me.

My mouth opens to scream, but lips tighten over mine, not letting it out.

The men shift, and I feel different hands, tongues, and mouths on me in different places. If I carefully studied how the scruff feels, how rough each hand feels, the tenor of each of their voices, I could make out who's where, but I don't care. I just want to be fucked so hard and passionately that every time a man tries to take what's mine from me again, I remember this moment. I remember how it feels to have four men worshipping me. How good it feels to be so desired and wanted.

And then everything changes.

I feel a hardness settling between my legs, and my heart rate quickens.

"I want you, Princess."

"We all do."

I suck in a breath. I'm worked up, wet, and so fucking ready for the next step, but these guys aren't going to take it. I have to.

I push my hips down and encompass his tip. He doesn't have to be asked twice—his cock pushes further inside me, making me cry out at how tight it feels. He feels enormous between my legs. He's not going to fit. I consider asking one of the other guys to fuck me first when I feel the return of a mouth over my nipple and another sucking my neck.

"Breathe, Princess. It will feel so damn good soon that you won't be able to believe you almost told us to stop."

I nod.

His cock slides all the way in, slamming into me with such force that I'm seeing stars, but I wouldn't have it any other way.

"Jesus, you're so fucking tight and wet and mine," he growls.

He takes his time sliding out and then torturously slowly back in, hitting every spot I didn't know existed. Each thrust fills me with pleasure. It's overwhelming, all the sensations in my body. I can't even register them all. Their touches, kisses, licks, moans, growls. All of it I'll replay later when my life is very different from now.

"God, I could fuck you all the damn time."

"Too bad it's my turn."

The man slams into me one more time, then pulls all

the way out. Another man enters me. This one is longer but thinner than the first, hitting even deeper new spots.

My body trembles as he fucks me, and another mouth sucks my clit while he's inside me. A cock is pushed against my mouth, and I suck it, loving having a man in two of my openings. My mind goes to what it would feel like to have a man in my ass as well, but then I shiver.

A chuckle strokes my ear. "You're not ready for that yet, Princess."

But I feel a finger press at my asshole, circling it and giving me a tiny taste of what it might feel like. The touch alone almost sends me over the edge again.

"I'm. Going. To—" A mouth captures mine, keeping me from being able to scream out my orgasm.

I'm so close, teetering on the edge of the most explosive orgasm, when I hear an intense growl. One that demands the attention of the entire room. It sucks all the air away. It rumbles louder than the sound of the music through the speakers.

There is no mistaking who just interrupted the most intense orgasm of my life.

19

RI

THE GUYS FLEE from my body left and right as I hear footsteps barreling through the room while I lie helpless on the pool table. I have no energy after being fucked to help, but I force myself to at least sit up. I need to get the blindfold off, which is stuck tightly on the top of my head.

Finally, I rip it off in time to see six feet of angry maleness approaching me. I don't know who his fury is directed at or why he's angry exactly, but it consumes everything as he rages toward me.

I can't tear my eyes away from him to look at the condition of the other guys. All I see is him.

As he gets closer, his eyes shift as he takes in my state, my nakedness. He's searching for something; I don't know what. It causes his eyes to darken into lust-filled orbs.

Then, without a word, he scoops me into his arm. Somehow, he cradles me with just his one arm. I expect him to throw me over his shoulder fireman style, but he doesn't. He holds me tight to his chest, and then he runs out of the room like we're being chased by a monster.

That's when I lose it.

How dare he tell me what I can and can't do with my body!

How dare he tell me who I can fuck!

How dare he pull me away from one of the best fucking experiences of my life!

I beat my hands against his chest and start kicking, wishing I knew how to defend myself, but he only grips me tighter. I don't know where he's taking me, but I hear voices, and he ducks into a room.

He kicks the door shut behind him and throws a lock with his shoulder. We're in a public bathroom, I realize through my anger.

"It's okay, Princess. You're safe. I've got you. I won't let them hurt you. You're just in shock." He grips me tighter, but finally, I kick free.

"What are you doing?" I scream.

"Saving you."

It hits me all at once. "Of course, you are, Hero. Of course you are." I run my hands through my hair with a frustrated grin. "I don't know why you decided to save me this time, but you got one little thing wrong."

He frowns, his brows pinching together. "What's that?"

"For once, I didn't need a hero."

"What did you need?"

"I needed you to let me save my damn self."

He cocks his head. "I don't understand. Those guys were raping you. I was doing you a favor. I saved you! I stopped them. I wasn't one of the men raping you."

I shake my head. *How dumb is he?* "I know, but you're mistaken. I wasn't being raped."

"You weren't?"

"No." I pull at the ends of my hair. I'd punch him if I knew how to throw a punch without injuring myself.

His mind thinks back to the scene he just walked in on.

"Think. Study the men in your mind. Look closer at what you saw."

His eyes shoot wide.

I nod as he finally realizes. "I asked the Retribution Kings to fuck me in order to help save me."

"What? How would fucking you save you?"

"My father wants to marry me off as a virgin. I may not be able to control who he marries me off too, but I can control whether I'm a virgin or not. You just ruined one of the best orgasms of my life."

He doesn't look the least bit sorry about that. He gives me a smug shrug as his apology.

It's then that I realize I'm still naked, but I don't hide my body. I'm too pissed off to do that.

"Wait...why do you think your father is going to marry you off when you're with us?"

I frown. Now I'm the one confused. "For one, I'm not with you. You guys don't care about me, especially you."

He winces.

"But I care about Odette. I've lost my memories, so the only way to help you is if you trade me for Odette or at least information about Odette. Whether my father has her or not is moot, he can get any information you want and even help get her back. He'll do it to get me back, I'm sure of it."

He stands there completely frozen, and I have no idea what is going through his head.

"What are you thinking?"

"You lost your memories?"

I nod.

"All of them?"

"Everything before I bumped into you on that elevator."

"And you're willing to sacrifice yourself to get my wife back?"

I nod.

His scowl deepens. It's almost like he doesn't believe me. Maybe he just hates me that much.

"Why do you think I hate you?" he asks.

"Because you do. You left me to Paxton and his crew to be married off and raped!"

"What if I didn't?"

"You did."

"Except that, I didn't."

My mouth gapes.

"I was the one who gave the order. I was the one who lead the charge. I was the one who was in most danger. I fought off guard after guard to keep them distracted instead of going after you when you escaped."

"Oh."

"Yea."

"But why?"

"Because I hate you."

"But you just said—"

"I never said I didn't hate you, just that I didn't leave you to be raped and tortured."

Except his eyes don't say he hates me at all, not even a little. Neither does his hard cock bulging through his pants.

Oh.

That's why he hates me.

He keeps saving the wrong girl. He keeps saving me instead of his wife.

And he hates himself for saving me.

He hates himself for wanting me, even though he would never cheat on his wife.

He hates that I'm not her.

I can't fault him for that.

But the way he's staring at me reminds me that I was on the brink of an orgasm and didn't get to finish. My body tingles all over, aching for a release that never came.

I part my lips as the feelings flood through me the longer he stares at me.

He pulls off his shirt and tosses it at me. "Put that on. I'll get you some more clothes as soon as I can."

"And you could go apologize to those guys."

"I'm not apologizing to those assholes. They shouldn't have been fucking you and filming you. That's more liable to piss your old man off."

I shrug and am about to slip on his shirt, but his scent overwhelms my nostrils. It's a fresh, sweet scent with just a touch of musk. I drag my eyes to look at Beckett. His hard chest makes my mouth water. I want nothing more than to run my tongue all over it, but I know he'd immediately send me to my father for a transgression like that.

I can't touch, but I can look.

I can finish the job that he denied me.

I let his shirt drop to the floor.

"What are you doing?"

I cup my breast in my hand. It feels heavy as I let my thumb perk my nipple.

Beckett freezes, his mouth falling ajar.

I ignore him and let my other hand trail down my stomach finding my clit just like the guys did earlier, rubbing in slow concentric circles.

"Stop." He finally regains his consciousness.

"I can't. I need this."

"Rialta, stop. Now." He never calls me Rialta. He rarely even calls me Ri. But I don't stop. I couldn't if I wanted to.

I spread my legs further apart as I slip a finger in. "God, I'm still wet."

Beckett turns to the door, jiggling the handle like he's trapped in here with a hungry lion.

"Shit, the lock's stuck." For some reason, he turns back around. It doesn't really matter. The view of his back is just as incredible as his front, and I'm two seconds away from coming.

But then he turns again, and his hooded gaze locks on my body. I realize I'd much rather have his eyes on me than not—such gorgeous, soulful eyes. His eyes beg me to stop while simultaneously needing this as much as I do.

I'm going to hell for this.

I'm torturing a man who loves another, devoted his life to another, married another.

But the need in me is too much. I need this release in order to function, to keep breathing.

Beckett doesn't fight me anymore. He just stares, even as I walk closer, my fingers pumping in and out while my thumb massages my clit.

I'm so close, so fucking close. I'm sure this will feel nothing like it might have with four hot guys all fucking my body simultaneously, but it will be enough to ensure I don't have blue balls the rest of the night. *Yes, I know women can't get blue balls, but whatever is the equivalent can't be good for me.*

I pump faster, my soft moans coming more frequently —almost there.

Beckett closes his eyes as if he's in physical pain. He

shoves his hand in the pocket of his jeans, most likely to keep from reaching out and touching me. It's a crucial mistake, one I take full advantage of.

The guys are great. Fucking any one of them would be incredible. Fucking them all at once was damn near magical. And yet, I still can't have the guy I really want.

The guy I hate.

The guy I don't deserve.

But maybe I can steal something that might rival what I could have felt with the guys. It could have made me realize that I just have a stupid crush on Beckett because he's smoking hot and has saved me multiple times. I would have fully moved on to Caius, or Hayes, or Gage, or even Lennox.

I lean forward and steal what Beckett stole from me. I press my lips to his and let go.

His eyes fly open in shock as I kiss him, but he doesn't jerk back. He doesn't kiss me full out either, but his hooded eyes tell me all the wicked ways he'd kiss me if I were his.

"Fuck," I yell into his mouth as I come. It's so much more than I expected it to be.

And I was so fucking wrong.

I thought the orgasm I would have had with the guys would have been the best one of my life; the one all others would chase.

Beckett stares at me with such intensity. Our lips are still pressed, and my cum is still on my fingers.

I just ruined everything, every guy for me ever. Beckett is that guy, and he's off-limits in so many ways. I just committed a grave sin, but it's one I'll never regret.

Because I just had the most intense, amazeballs

orgasm. The only way I can ever imagine it being topped is if Beckett fucked me himself. He'll never do that.

The flame of rage returns in full force in his eyes. Whatever retribution he has planned for me will be worth it. His glare intensifies, and I gulp.

I hope it'll be worth it.

20

BECKETT

SHE FUCKING KISSED ME. *How dare she!*

Out of everything I've experienced—losing an arm, getting shot at, tortured, losing friends, running for my life —*how does her kissing me feel like the worst thing that's ever happened?*

Because I liked it.

I don't hate her; I hate me.

I'm married. I love Odette, even though I'm not sure she loves me back. I'm not a cheater, and yet, I've kissed this woman twice now.

No, I didn't kiss her. She kissed me! I didn't kiss her back. I just fucking enjoyed it like the sick fuck I am.

I don't know why I felt something when Ri kissed me, probably just typical male hormones reacting to a naked woman kissing him. Of course, I enjoyed her kiss.

But why did I react so strongly when I thought she was being raped by four guys? I was about to level the city; that's how much rage I felt. Then being alone with her in this bathroom is when everything shifted. We have a connection. I don't even know if it's romantic—actually, I know it's not. It's something deeper, more sinister, like we share half of the devil's soul inside us both.

It doesn't mean I don't want Odette. It doesn't mean that once I get her back, I won't spend the rest of my life groveling trying to get her forgiveness. But it does mean I have to reconcile with the fact that I share something with Ri, even if I don't understand what that connection means.

"Get dressed," I order.

Finally, Ri complies. She grabs my shirt lying on the floor and slips it on. It at least covers her breasts and ass, but not much else. Her nipples still press against the thin fabric, and I can make out every curve on her body. It's an improvement, but not much.

"Come on, we should check that the guys aren't too upset that I kicked their asses," I say.

That comment earns me a smile. "How exactly did you take all four of them out while only having one good arm anyway? I didn't think you were that good."

"Oh, I'm that good, baby." I wink. Plus, the guys were too concerned with sticking their dicks in her to see me coming. And I was full of rage. I'll just be happy if I didn't do any permanent damage.

We walk back into the club VIP room, unsure of what we'll find.

Four sets of eyes meet us as we step into the room. They are all sitting on various pieces of furniture, nursing their wounds.

Caius is sitting on the edge of the pool table with a bag of ice pressed against his jaw. Lennox is lying on one of the couches with a glare that tells me he's going to pay me back for the kick to his ribs. Hayes found a glass of scotch and is drinking it with a bad gash under his eye, his glasses broken lying on his lap while he sits on the other couch. And Gage is sitting on an armrest with a bag of ice pressed against his forehead.

All of the masks and disguises are gone. None of them are wearing shirts, but at least they all have their dicks in their pants. They all look at me like they want to kill me, though. I probably just fucked up any remaining chance at becoming their permanent leader, not that I give a damn.

"You okay?" they all simultaneously ask Ri.

She gives me a dirty look. "Yea, I'm okay." She walks over to Caius, slowly. I assume their interactions are going to be awkward and forced, considering how I found them before.

Instead, Ri wraps her arms around Caius's neck. "Thank you."

Caius removes the bag of ice and wraps his arms around her, his cheeks pinking.

"All of you," Ri adds as she smiles at each of them.

I stiffen, hating how she's thanking all of them for fucking her. Something they all gladly got enjoyment out of. It wasn't like it was a hardship for any of them.

Hayes gets up and picks her clothes up off the floor before handing them to Ri.

She nods with a smile and then starts slipping back into her jeans and jacket over my shirt.

The rest of the guys start putting their shirts back on until I'm the only one shirtless.

"What do you want us to do about the video?" Gage asks.

Lennox is the only one who hasn't approached her or spoken. He hangs back, quiet, letting his anger fester.

"I say burn it." All eyes fly to me, and they might as well be daggers.

"I didn't ask you," Gage snarls.

We all look to Ri, whose head is now resting against Caius's chest with his arm tucked around her shoulders. Her face pales as she thinks about it.

"Send it to my father."

"No," I bark.

"Yes," she hisses.

"It's too dangerous. You don't know how your father is going to react. He'll punish you and do everything he can to find every person in that video. You are putting them all at risk."

"Like you care about our safety," Lennox snarks.

I snap my head to him. "Maybe you shouldn't have been so rough with her, and I wouldn't have mistaken your actions as rape."

Lennox stands up and marches toward me, puffing his chest. "Maybe you should have been here instead of crying because you aren't enough to save your wife."

I punch him.

"Enough!" Ri yells before I get another swing in.

I step back. I was done with this asshole anyway.

Ri looks at me with a threat in her eyes. "It's not your decision to make, Hero; it's mine." She looks back to Gage. "Send it to my father."

He nods.

No one else speaks up. I guess they all thought it was a good idea, or they wouldn't have gone through with it in the first place.

"Let's get out of here. Get a hotel for tonight, and we can figure out what the hell we are going to do in the morning," Caius says, taking charge. Apparently, after I beat their asses, he's decided he's the better leader. It doesn't make sense to me, but whatever. I'm clearly the best fighter.

Caius leads Ri out of the room with his arm still around her. I follow after, and the rest walk behind me. We almost make it to the outside door when a voice stops us dead in our tracks.

"Time's up," Ares says.

My heart thumps slowly and time stills. In all the chaos, I forgot that it's been a week. A week since I got married. A week without Odette. A week since I made a deal with the Phantom Brotherhood that I was never going to honor.

But our only shot of getting out of here is to pretend the deal is still on.

"Why else do you think we came to your club?" I ask, taking a shot that this is a Phantom club as I turn to face Ares.

The rest of my guys fall behind me, ready for a fight. I guess they still honor me as their leader after all.

"You came here to tell me that the deal is done?"

"Princess and I got married last night."

"Doesn't look that way to me," Ares gestures to where Ri is still snuggled under Caius's arm.

I shrug casually. "I like to share."

Ares narrows his eyes, not believing me. I whistle and snap my fingers at Ri like she's a dog, not a woman.

To my surprise, she obediently walks out from under Caius's arm and under mine. She must realize the danger we are all in. I grab her chin and kiss her sloppily, licking over every inch of her lips like I own them.

She growls back and fights back with her own rough assault against my mouth.

I grope her then, spinning her back against my front.

Ares looks amused.

"How'd you break her so quickly? I thought she'd take years to break."

I feel her pulse racing under my fingertips at Ares's words.

"Easy, Princess, his time will come," I breathe against her ear so only she can hear.

"Maybe I'll show you after our deal is done," I say to Ares.

"Speaking of, did you arrange for my agreement with Corsi, or do I have to kill someone you love?"

"Did you already?" I ask, suspiciously.

"I haven't touched anyone who is yours. If I did, I knew you'd never cut me into the deal."

He's right about that.

"What did happen to that fiancée of yours?"

"I took care of her," I say with a wicked laugh, hating myself even more. It's why I need Odette back. I'm a better person when she's here.

Ares grins. "So our deal with Corsi?"

This isn't how I wanted this to go. This isn't what I had planned. But this is how they are all going to find out what I've done.

We all feel the shift of darkness descend into the room. There are dozens of dangerous, soulless men here, but the temperature doesn't drop until he enters. He's on a different level, more dangerous because he has no limits to what he will do for power—including selling his own daughter for more of it.

"You know no one can make a deal with me on your behalf, Ares," Vincent Corsi says.

Then he shoots Ares in the head.

21

RI

"DAD?"

My father lowers his gun after firing into Ares's skull. He doesn't glance my way.

Beckett's arm is still wrapped around me. "Don't look," he whispers.

But of course, I look.

Ares is lying on the ground with his brains blown out and blood oozing in a large puddle around his head. The rest of his men stand behind his body in postures of submission. They aren't going to fire back at my father. They aren't going to attack. They are going to let my father kill their leader without retaliation. They know if they fight back, they'll be next.

My father starts to walk back out of the club.

"Rialta," he says in a low, commanding voice.

This is it, the moment I've been dreading. *Am I strong enough to just walk away with my father, to sacrifice myself for someone I don't even know?*

But then I feel Beckett's heart beating against my back. He'll never survive without her. Odette may not love him, but she's his everything. *When he gets her back, how could she not fall madly in love with him?* I may hate him most of the time, but dammit, one of us deserves a happily ever after. It won't be me, but he can get one.

I start to move, but Beckett's grip on me tightens. The guys block me from Corsi.

How stupid are they? You don't stand up to my father and live to talk about it.

"Beckett, thank you for ensuring my daughter's safe return. The information you need is waiting for you at the Retribution Kings' headquarters." My father's gray eyebrow raises, and his lips move in a sinister curl, while he waits to see what Beckett is going to do.

"Of course. You can count on us to bring her back to you anytime," Beckett says, and then he releases me. He doesn't exactly shove me into my father's waiting arms, but he doesn't protect me either.

The rest of the guys stare at me with various states of concern. But I nod at Caius, and he slowly takes a step back. The rest follow suit until they've parted a path for me directly to my father. I don't look at any of them as I walk to my father's side.

I can't count on them anymore. They can't save me. There is nothing any of them can do. But I can't blame them either; I'm the one who agreed to this. They aren't forcing me. The only thing I can be upset with is that Beckett apparently already talked to my father. He knew he was coming. He could have warned me.

My father places his hand on the small of my back when I reach him, and then he starts walking. I keep pace next to him as we walk toward the back of the club with his security guards protecting us. When we reach the door, I consider looking back, but I don't. I have to forget about them, even though they're my everything. Literally, because I can't remember any time before them.

I walk through the door. *They're my past now.*

My father guides me into the back of a car, and the driver in the front seat starts driving.

I don't bother to put my seatbelt on. I'd rather be dead than face what comes next.

No, Beckett showed me that I can feel. I want to live.

I put my seatbelt on.

My father doesn't speak as we drive. I try to remember anything about him, but it doesn't take much to know that he's a cruel man who is used to getting his way. I don't open my mouth to ask questions.

I just hope that Beckett has what he needs to get Odette back. Later tonight, he'll be driving to pick her up, and they'll share a happy reunion. That's what I focus on with every block we drive down.

My father pulls his phone out of his pocket. He pulls something up and then places the phone on the seat between us.

I stare wide-eyed at a video.

He presses play, but I already know what the video is.

It's the middle of the video with all four men holding onto me. Gage is kissing me. Hayes is fondling my breasts. Lennox is spreading my legs. And Caius is driving inside me. It's fucking hot and would bring back happy memories of that night if it wasn't for the fact that my sick father is watching.

I press pause and look away.

He takes the phone and puts it back in his jacket pocket as we drive through the city streets. There isn't much traffic, so wherever we are going, we are making record time.

"Don't think I don't know it was your idea."

"Looks like I was being forced. They were holding my arms and legs, and I was blindfolded." Inside, I do a victory lap, happy to have pissed my father off.

"You'll be punished for your indiscretion, as will your friends."

I swallow. He has no idea who the guys are. The video is edited to make it even grainier and darker. Between that, the lighting, and the masks, it's almost impossible to tell who the men are. I can barely make out the different guys. If my father suspected it was the Retribution Kings, he would have killed them all back there.

His face shifts into sadistic anger that festers the entire ride. Whatever my punishment will be, it was worth it.

The driver pulls into an underground garage right in front of an elevator. I'm nervous that something is going to be expected of me that I can't remember. That my father will realize I don't have any memories and use that to his advantage. I don't want him to know, at least until I figure why I've forgotten and if he has anything to do with it.

My father steps out of the car, as do I, and then we walk into the elevator. He presses a button for the top floor, and the elevator rises.

The doors open into a penthouse suite, and we both step out.

I open my mouth to speak, but my father beats me to it. "Sleep, Rialta. I'll deal with you in the morning."

He walks off before I can say anything.

That's it?

He's just going to leave me unguarded? Could it be this easy to escape?

But then I notice guards filing around me.

"This way, Miss Corsi," one of the guards says, like I'm not a prisoner in my father's home.

I follow him up the stairs to a large bedroom with a corner view of the city. It's incredible, but it doesn't spark any memories. *How many nights have I slept in this room?*

"If you need anything, I'll be right outside your door," he says.

I nod, and he leaves me alone.

I walk around the room, my hand trailing over the stark white fabrics of the bed and dresser. The single frame of me with my parents on the nightstand. The light gray walls. None of it sparks anything, but when I head into the bathroom and see the toiletries and closet full of clothes my size, I know that I've stayed here plenty before.

I slip on a pair of my old pajama bottoms but leave Beckett's T-shirt on. I brush my teeth and climb into bed. I want to fight, but I'm far too tired. I grab the collar of the shirt and take a deep breath, inhaling Beckett's musk.

I smile. My future may be fucked, but any minute now, he'll be reuniting with his love, and I can't pretend that doesn't make me happy.

Even if my heart does ache that he'll never be mine.

22

RI

THE NEXT DAY, I'm confined to my room. A guard brings me a couple of bottles of water and celery throughout the day, but that's all I get.

No real food.

No TV.

No cell phone.

No internet.

No books.

Nothing to entertain me.

Apparently, this is the first part of my punishment—lock me up like I'm Rapunzel.

I lie on my bed with my stomach growling as I toss a scrunchie up and down. I'm still wearing Beckett's shirt, and my daydreams have been flooded with nothing but Beckett and Odette's reuniting.

My latest daydream is of Beckett riding in on a horse, slaying the dragon that was holding her hostage, and they immediately ride off into the sunset together. *Okay, I know it's not realistic, but the realistic dreams are too emotional. I* feel nothing but heart stabbing pain when I think of them living happily ever after for real.

Beckett and Odette—their names practically rhyme. It's like fate brought them together. They were made for each other. I can just imagine how adorably cute they are strolling down a beach hand in hand.

I sit up. I have to stop thinking about them. I did my part. Now I have to start figuring out how to survive long enough to escape.

My door opens suddenly, and a man holds a large black garment bag.

"You have two hours to get ready." The guard walks in and hangs the bag in my closet. "If you're late, Mr. Corsi says he'll take it out on your friends."

I sigh. "And does Mr. Corsi expect me to get ready and attend whatever party tonight without passing out? Because if so, I'm going to need more than a couple of pieces of celery."

The guard smirks. He steps out and returns with a covered plate and another large bottle of water.

Thank god.

He sets my plate on my nightstand and then leaves.

I rush to uncover the plate and frown. There are four pieces of celery and a couple of raisins. I grab a piece of celery and fling it at the door.

"Jerk!"

I immediately realize my mistake and pick up the piece of celery off the floor. I eat it quickly, along with every morsel of food on the plate. I need every ounce of energy I can afford. My father's trying to keep me weak, so I can't fight back.

I walk to the closet to check out my dictated outfit. I

unzip the garment bag and find a black dress with thin straps at the top, cutouts around the middle, and it seems to swirl in a long train at the back. There's some jewelry included—a bracelet, earrings, and a tiara.

I sigh. *What is it with grown men thinking a twenty-year-old woman needs a tiara?*

As much as I want to refuse it all, I won't. I have to pick my battles. I'll play the dutiful daughter who does everything her father tells her, then strike when he least expects it.

And I won't put my friends, as my father said, at risk. I owe them that for a little longer. So I spend the next two hours turning myself into a sleek princess.

———

I feel lightheaded as I take the chauffeur's hand and climb out of the back of the limo. I understand now why my father didn't let me eat today. This dress is tiny around my waist. I was barely able to squeeze into it as it is.

My father steps up next to me as we walk into the building. "I'm glad you remember your place, Rialta."

I don't respond but just walk obediently next to him.

"Right this way, sir," a man in a tux says as soon as we enter.

I notice that several guards instantly fall in line behind us and in front of us as we walk through the building, so much so that I can't tell where we are going. I have no idea what this event tonight is about, only that I'm in a very formal dress and my father is in a tux. Maybe if I had memories from before, I'd know what type of events my father usually requires me to attend this dressed up.

Double doors are opened in front of us, and we all march into a grand ballroom. There are large chandeliers hanging and lighting all the faces of the men and women waiting. It doesn't take much for me to realize who are sitting at all the tables. I recognize a few members of Mayhem and Phantom Brotherhood as we walk by. This a gathering of the gangs, crews, and dangerous monsters.

I expect us to stop at a table, but we don't. We keep walking straight onto a stage. The guards part to either side of the stage, showing their presence but not holding anyone's attention. No, that honor goes to my father and me as we walk together toward the center of the stage.

The lights dim in the room, and a bright spotlight is shone on us, so I can barely make out the faces of the crowd. I have no idea what is going on, but I stand tall with my shoulders back. I won't show fear no matter what happens.

"Thank you all for gathering. As you know, we have several important things to discuss. First, I'd like you to celebrate the safe return of my daughter, Rialta Corsi."

The crowd breaks out into applause and cheers at my father's words.

On the other hand, my father shows no signs of happiness at my safe return. When the cheering dies down, he continues. "Now, for the less than happy news. As you all know, Rialta was set to be married to Nicolo Ricci on her twenty-first birthday."

The room falls into pin-drop silence, and I'm terrified they can all hear my heart beating in panic. *Is my father going to move up the wedding?*

When is my twenty-first birthday? Is it today?

"But it is with a heavy heart that I have to report that Nicolo has been murdered."

Instant murmuring breaks out around the room. I glance over at my father, who once again shows no emotion. I have no idea what he's planning next.

"My daughter's safety has been at risk over this last week, but the Retribution Kings ensured her safe return. And they helped me create a plan for how to keep her safe forever."

Dread fills me as my father speaks. *The Retribution Kings helped my father create this plan?* He means Beckett. *What did Beckett do?*

"My daughter is in need of a husband. One who will keep her safe."

I roll my eyes. A husband who will keep me safe, my ass. He only cares about keeping his power and ensuring my husband controls me.

"With such a prize as my daughter at stake, there are bound to be fights breaking out. So to ensure the best man for the job wins, I've devised a game. It will keep my daughter safe and prevent fighting amongst ourselves outside of the game. The winner gets to marry my daughter."

My nostrils flare as my breathing hardens. My father is going to host a game, and the winner gets to marry me. And Beckett was the one who came up with the idea.

My hands fist as I try to restrain myself. Beckett better have gotten Odette back and convinced her that she loves him. That's the only way I won't murder him for this.

"I'm sure you are wondering what the rules are, but that will have to wait. For now, know this—any man here can enter, only one will win. If you enter and lose...well, I don't recommend losing." He smirks.

The crowd chuckles at his morbid joke. Then, my

father glares at everyone in the crowd, and the room once again falls silent.

"Enter however many men from your crew that you dare, but you must follow my rules. If you don't, there will be consequences." He snaps his fingers, and an image appears on a screen behind us of Ares lying dead on the floor.

After a moment, my father nods for the screen to turn off, and the image disappears. I'm surprised he doesn't pull up the video of the guys fucking me, but maybe he hasn't actually identified who's in the video. Or he wants everyone to think I'm still the obedient virgin daughter.

"There are cards on your table. If you would like to enter the game, sign your name in blood, and then bring your card to the stage. Place it in the bowl in my beautiful daughter's hands."

A guard walks over and places a gold bowl into my shaky hands.

I still can't see out into the crowd as the spotlight blinds me, and the room remains mostly dark. But I can hear murmurs around the room, trying to understand what twisted game my father is playing. These men are idiots if they don't realize Vincent is most likely enticing them into a game where he can kill off his enemies without retaliation because it's all part of the game. They should only enter if they are on Vincent's good side and have a legitimate shot at winning.

The first man walks onto the stage, and the crowd cheers him on. I stand frozen, hating that I'm nothing more than a prop. My father dressed me up like a sexy princess to entice these men into playing his twisted game.

The man winks at me as he places the first card in the

bowl I'm holding. The man is young, cocky, and destined to lose. I don't have to worry about this asshole becoming my husband.

Once the first man places his card, the floodgates open. Men file onto the stage boasting about how they are the strongest, the handsomest, the most dangerous, and how they will win and claim me as their wife.

I see members of Mayhem, Phantom Brotherhood, and plenty of other men of all ages enter the game. All I can think about is how stupid they are and how they're walking into a trap.

But I'm just as trapped as they are.

They think I'm their princess, their property to win, an opinionless prize. They have no clue who I really am. I may have no clue who I really am either, but I'm about to find out. I'll be their princess for now, but soon I'll be the one bringing them all to their knees.

My father may have created this game, but I'm going to find a way to insert my own power. I can tame men, even the most dangerous in this room.

*No...*My breath catches.

Caius walks onto the stage with his gorgeous blonde hair, tall and proud. He walks right up to me with his card signed in blood in his hand.

"Caius, no," I whisper, daring not to say more. As much as Caius winning and us marrying would be the best outcome, he doesn't have anything my father wants. He has no power, no control over a crew or region. There is nothing he can give my father. He'll lose, and he'll have to pay whatever price my father decides.

"I owe you a life."

"No, you already gave me one."

His hand hovers over the bowl. I grab his wrist, trying to get him to stop, but he opens his hand, and the card drops in.

Shit.

I release his hand, trying not to draw any more attention to Caius. I don't want my father to target him because I favor him.

"Don't let the others enter," I whisper.

Caius gives me a stiff nod and then walks off the stage.

A stream of unknown men file on the stage and drop cards into my bowl, but now I'm in a haze.

Caius entered.

I won't let my heart hope for even a minute that he's going to win. He won't. But it will be nice to have a friend nearby, even if I can't rely on him to help me.

I turn to see what asshole is entering next when I see Beckett walk up onto the stage.

Beckett—my heart thumps his name.

Did he come on stage to boast with my father? It was his idea after all.

I grit my teeth and glare at him. Now I'm going to have to suffer through whatever twisted game my father has planned. I'm sure I'll have to participate far more than I want, be traded around to the most dangerous men like a trading card, somehow survive, only to be forced into a marriage to a man who will rape me, treat me like an object, until I drown myself in drugs or alcohol.

Beckett doesn't walk over to my father. Instead, he walks to me.

I frown, not understanding.

"Did you find Odette?"

He doesn't answer me, but I see a card in his hand— the same card as everyone else, marked with his blood.

He's not going to enter. He can't. He loves Odette. He wouldn't want to marry me.

But he drops the card into the bowl. I watch as it falls in slow motion, mixing with the other cards.

I quickly glance back up and really look at him without my own anger masking him. His eyes are red and puffy, his face drained of color, and his nostrils flare every time he takes a deep breath.

There is only one reason he would ever enter this game.

My heart sinks.

Odette's dead.

I want to hold him and punch him at the same time. I'm pretty sure that's how he feels, too, based on his fist continually clenching and bulging a vein in his forearm.

He's not entering because he wants to marry me or save me like Caius is doing. He's entering to get revenge for Odette's death. I don't know who he blames—my father, the Phantom Brotherhood, me, or someone else, but the need for revenge is clear on his face.

It's then that I realize that Beckett didn't give my father the idea before he turned me over. He gave it to him after he realized Odette was dead. To punish me. To hurt me. To make me suffer. Or to give him an opportunity to fuck with my father or find the man who killed her. Beckett isn't on my side.

But my heart speeds, because maybe he could win. Maybe I want him to win. Maybe I could love him. Those maybes are all possible.

The more impossible outcome is him loving me after losing the love of his life. *Can he love someone he hates?*

He leans in and whispers, "I call these the Retribution Games. I'm about to kill everyone that had anything to do with her death. Sorry if a little blood splatters on your pretty tiara, Princess."

Then he disappears back into the darkness, and I'm left standing on the stage horrified for my future while desperate for a man set on revenge. Beckett won't save me, but then again, I didn't ask for a hero.

"Game on, Hero."

———

Thank you for reading Mistaken Hero! I hope you enjoyed it! Beckett and Ri's story continues in Forbidden Princess!

JOIN ELLA'S NEWSLETTER & NEVER MISS A SALE OR NEW RELEASE → ellamiles.com/freebooks

Love swag boxes & signed books?
SHOP MY STORE → store.ellamiles.com

ALSO BY ELLA MILES

LIES SERIES:

Lies We Share: A Prologue

Vicious Lies

Desperate Lies

Fated Lies

Cruel Lies

Dangerous Lies

Endless Lies

SINFUL TRUTHS:

Sinful Truth #1

Twisted Vow #2

Reckless Fall #3

Tangled Promise #4

Fallen Love #5

Broken Anchor #6

TRUTH OR LIES:

Taken by Lies #1

Betrayed by Truths #2

Trapped by Lies #3

Stolen by Truths #4

Possessed by Lies #5

Consumed by Truths #6

DIRTY SERIES:

Dirty Obsession

Dirty Addiction

Dirty Revenge

Dirty: The Complete Series

ALIGNED SERIES:

Aligned: Volume 1 (Free Series Starter)

Aligned: Volume 2

Aligned: Volume 3

Aligned: Volume 4

Aligned: The Complete Series Boxset

UNFORGIVABLE SERIES:

Heart of a Thief

Heart of a Liar

Heart of a Prick

Unforgivable: The Complete Series Boxset

MAYBE, DEFINITELY SERIES:

Maybe Yes

Maybe Never

Maybe Always

Definitely Yes

Definitely No

Definitely Forever

STANDALONES:

Pretend I'm Yours

Pretend We're Over

Finding Perfect

Savage Love

Too Much

Not Sorry

Hate Me or Love Me: An Enemies to Lovers Romance Collection

ABOUT THE AUTHOR

Ella Miles writes steamy romance, including everything from dark suspense romance that will leave you on the edge of your seat to contemporary romance that will leave you laughing out loud or crying. Most importantly, she wants you to feel everything her characters feel as you read.

Ella is currently living her own happily ever after near the Rocky Mountains with her high school sweetheart husband. Her heart is also taken by her goofy five year old black lab who is scared of everything, including her own shadow.

Ella is a USA Today Bestselling Author & Top 50 Bestselling Author.

Stalk Ella at:
www.ellamiles.com
ella@ellamiles.com

www.ingramcontent.com/pod-product-compliance
Lightning Source LLC
Chambersburg PA
CBHW021138190726
48288CB00008B/2725